Voltaire

Zadig or the Book of Fate

Outlook

Voltaire

Zadig or the Book of Fate

1. Auflage | ISBN: 978-3-73262-488-1

Erscheinungsort: Frankfurt am Main, Deutschland

Erscheinungsjahr: 2018

Outlook Verlag GmbH, Frankfurt.

ZADIG;

OR, THE

Book of Fate.

AN

Oriental HISTORY,

1

Translated from the

French ORIGINAL

OF

M^{R.} *V O L T A I R E .*

———Quo fata trahunt, retrahuntque sequamur.
Per varios casus, per tot discrimina rerum,
Tendimus in Latium. ——— V_{IRG.}

L O N D O N :

Printed for I_{OHN} B_{RINDLEY}, Bookseller
to His Royal Highness the Prince of
Wales, in *New Bond-Street.*

MDCCXLIX.

THE

D E D I C A T I O N

TO THE

S_{ULTANA} *SHERAA,*

BY

SADI.

The 18th of the Month *Scheval*, in the
Year of the *Hegira*, 837.

T hou Joy of ev'ry Eye! Thou Torment of every Heart! Thou Intellectual Light! I do not kiss the Dust of thy Feet; because thou seldom art seen out of the Seraglio, and when thou art, thou walkest only on the Carpets of *Iran*, or on Beds of Roses.

I here present you with a Translation of the Work of an ancient *Sage*, who having the Happiness of living free from all Avocations, thought proper, by Way of Amusement, to write the History of *Zadig*; a Performance, that comprehends in it more Instruction than, 'tis possible, you may at first be aware of. I beg you would indulge me so far as to read it over, and then pass your impartial Judgment upon it: For notwithstanding you are in the Bloom of your Life; tho' ev'ry Pleasure courts you; tho' you are Nature's Darling, and have internal Qualities in proportion to your Beauty; tho' the World resounds your Praises from Morning till Night, and consequently you must have a just Title to a superior Degree of Understanding than the rest of your Sex; Yet your Wit is no ways flashy; Your Taste is refin'd, and I have had the Honour to hear you talk more learnedly than the wisest *Dervise*, with his venerable Beard, and pointed Bonnet: You are discreet, and yet not mistrustful; you are easy, but not weak; you are beneficent with Discretion; you love your Friends, and create yourself no Enemies. Your most sprightly Flights borrow no Graces from Detraction; you never speak a misbecoming Word, nor do an ill- natur'd Action, tho' 'tis always in your Power. In a Word, your Soul is as spotless as your Person. You have, moreover, a little Fund of Philosophy, which gives me just Grounds to hope that you'll relish this Historical Performance better than any other Lady of your Quality would do.

It was originally compos'd in the *Chaldean* Language, to which both you and my self are perfect Strangers. It was translated, however, into *Arabic*, for the Amusement of the celebrated Sultan Ouloug-beg. It first appear'd in Public, when the *Arabian* and *Persian* Tales of One Thousand and One Nights, and One Thousand and One Days, were most in Vogue: Ouloug chose rather to entertain himself with the Adventures of *Zadig*. The Sultanas indeed were more fond of the former. How can you, said the judicious Ouloug, be so partial, as to prefer a Set of Tales, that are no ways interesting or instructive, to a Work, that has a Variety of Beauties to recommend it? Oh! replied the Sultanas, the less Sense there is in them, the more they are in Taste; and the less their Merit, the greater their Commendation.

I flatter my self, thou Patroness of Wisdom, that thou wilt not copy after those thoughtless Sultanas, but give into the Sentiments of Oⁿʟᴏᴜɢ. I am in hopes likewise, when you are tir'd with the Conversation of such as make those senseless Romances abovemention'd their favourite Amusements, you will vouchsafe to listen for one Minute or two, to the Dictates of solid Sense. Had you been *Thalestris* in the Days of *Scander*, the Son of *Philip*; had you been the Queen of *Sheba*, in the Reign of *Solomon*, those Kings would have been proud to have taken a Tour to visit you.

May the Celestial Virtues grant, that your Pleasures may meet with no Interruption; your Charms know no Decay; and may your Felicity be everlasting!

SADI.

THE

Approbation.

I, Who have subscrib'd my Name hereto, ambitious of being thought a Man of Wit and Learning, have perus'd this Mᴀɴᴜsᴄʀɪᴘᴛ, which I find, to my great Mortification, amusing, moral, philosophical, and fit to be read, even by those who have an utter Aversion to Romances; for which Reason, I have depretiated it, as it deserves, and have in direct Terms told the Cᴀᴅɪ-Lᴇsǫᴜɪᴇʀ, that 'tis a most detestable Performance.

THE

CONTENTS.

ZADIG:

AN
Oriental History.

CHAP. I.

The Blind Eye.

I n the Reign of King *Moabdar*, there was a young Man, a Native of *Babylon*, by name *Zadig*; who was not only endowed by Nature with an uncommon Genius, but born of illustrious Parents, who bestowed on him an Education no ways inferior to his Birth. Tho' rich and young, he knew how to give a Check to his Passions; he was no ways self-conceited; he didn't always act up to the strictest Rules of Reason himself, and knew how to look on the Foibles of others, with an Eye of Indulgence. Every one was surpriz'd to find, that notwithstanding he had such a Fund of Wit, he never insulted; nay, never so much as rallied any of his Companions, for that Tittle Tattle, which was so vague and empty, so noisy and confus'd; for those rash Reflections, those illiterate Conclusions, and those insipid Jokes; and, in short, for that Flow of unmeaning Words, which was call'd polite Conversation in *Babylon*. He had learned from the first Book of *Zoroaster*, that Self-love is like a Bladder full blown, which when once prick'd, discharges a kind of petty Tempest. *Zadig*, in particular, never boasted of his Contempt of the Fair Sex, or of his Facility to make Conquests amongst them. He was of a generous Spirit; insomuch, that he was not afraid of obliging even an ungrateful Man; strictly adhering to that wise Maxim of *Zoroaster*. *When you are eating, throw an Offal to the Dogs that are under the Table, lest they should be tempted to bite you.* He was as wise as he could well be wish'd; since he was fond of no Company, but such as were distinguish'd for Men of Sense. As he was well-grounded, in all the Sciences of the antient *Chaldeans*, he was no Stranger to those Principles of Natural Philosophy, which were then known: And understood as much of Metaphysics as any one in all Ages after him; that is to say, he knew little or nothing of the Matter. He was firmly convinc'd, that the Year consisted of 365 Days and an half, tho' directly repugnant to the new Philosophy of the Age he liv'd in; and that the Sun was situated in the Center of the Earth; And when the Chief Magi told him, with an imperious Air, that he maintain'd erroneous Principles; and that it was an Indignity offered to the Government under which he liv'd, to imagine the Sun should roll round its own Axis, and that the Year consisted of twelve Months, he knew how to sit still and quiet, without shewing the least Tokens of Resentment or Contempt.

As *Zadig* was immensely rich, and had consequently Friends without Number; and as he was a Gentleman of a robust Constitution, and remarkably handsome; as he was endowed with a plentiful Share of ready and inoffensive Wit: And, in a Word, as his Heart was perfectly sincere and open, he imagin'd himself, in some Measure, qualified to be perfectly happy. For which Purpose he determin'd to marry a gay young Lady (one *Semira* by name) whose Beauty, Birth and Fortune, render'd her the most desirable Person in all *Babylon*. He had a sincere Affection for her, grounded on Honour, and *Semira* conceiv'd as tender a Passion for him. They were just upon the critical Minute of a mutual Conjunction in the Bands of Matrimony, when, as they were walking Hand in Hand together towards one of the Gates of *Babylon*, under the Shade of a Row of Palm-trees, that grew on the Banks of the River *Euphrates*, they were beset by a Band of Ruffians, arm'd with Sabres, Bows and Arrows. They were the Guards, it seems, of young *Orcan* (Nephew of a certain Minister of State) whom the Parasites, kept by his Uncle, had buoy'd up with a Permission to do, with Impunity, whatever he thought proper. This young Rival, tho' he had none of those internal Qualities to boast of that *Zadig* had, yet he imagin'd himself a Man of more Power; and for that Reason, was perfectly outrageous to see the other preferr'd before him. This Fit of Jealousy, the Result of mere Vanity, prompted him to think that he was deeply in Love with the fair *Semira*; and fir'd with that amorous Notion, he was determin'd to take her away from *Zadig*, by Dint of Arms. The Ravishers rush'd rudely upon her, and in the Transport of their Rage, drew the Blood of a Beauty, the Sight of whose Charms would have soften'd the very Tigers of Mount *Imaüs*. The injur'd Lady rent the very Heavens with her Exclamations. Where's my dear Husband, she cried? They have torn me from the Arms of the only Man whom I adore. She never reflected on the Danger to which she was expos'd; her sole Concern was for her beloved *Zadig*. At the same Time, he defended her, like a Lover, and a Man of Integrity and Courage. With the Assistance only of two domestic Servants, he put those Sons of Violence to Flight, and conducted *Semira*, bloody as she was, and in fainting Fits, to her own House. No sooner was she come to her self, but she fix'd her lovely Eyes on her Dear Deliverer. O *Zadig*, said she, I love thee as affectionately, as if I were actually thy Bride: I love thee, as the Man, to whom I owe my Life, and what is dearer to me, the Preservation of my Honour. No Heart sure could be more deeply smitten than that of *Semira*. Never did the Lips of the fairest Creature living utter softer Sounds; never did the most enamoured Lady breathe such tender Sentiments of Love and Gratitude for his signal Service; never, in short, did the most affectionate Bride express such Transports of Joy for the fondest Husband. Her Wounds, however, were but very superficial, and she was soon recover'd. *Zadig* receiv'd a Wound that was much more dangerous: An unlucky Arrow had graz'd one of his Eyes, and the Orifice was deep. *Semira* was incessant in her Prayers to the Gods that they might restore her *Zadig*. Her Eyes were Night and Day overwhelm'd with Tears. She waited with Impatience for the happy Moment, when those of *Zadig* might dart their Fires upon her; but alas! the wounded Eye grew so inflam'd and swell'd, that she was terrified to the last Degree. She sent as far as *Memphis* for *Hermes*, the celebrated Physician there, who instantly attended his new Patient with a numerous Retinue. Upon his first Visit, he peremptorily declared that *Zadig* would lose his Eye; and foretold not only the Day, but the very Hour when that woful Disaster would befal him. Had it been, said that Great Man, his right Eye, I could have administred an infallible Specific; but as it is, his Misfortune is beyond the Art of Man to cure. Tho' all *Babylon* pitied the hard Case of *Zadig*, they equally stood astonish'd at the profound Penetration of *Hermes*. Two Days after the Imposthume broke, without any Application, and *Zadig* soon after was perfectly recover'd. *Hermes* thereupon wrote a very long and elaborate Treatise, to prove that his Wound ought not to have been heal'd. *Zadig*, however, never thought it worth his while to peruse his learned Lucubrations; but, as soon as ever he could get abroad, determin'd to pay the Lady a Visit, who had testified such uncommon Concern for his Welfare, and for whose Sake alone he wish'd for the Restoration of his Sight. *Semira* he found had been out of Town for three Days; but was inform'd, by the bye, that his intended Spouse, having conceived an implacable Aversion to a one-ey'd Man, was that very Night to be married to *Orcan*. At this unexpected ill News, poor *Zadig* was perfectly thunder-struck: He laid his Disappointment so far to Heart, that in a short Time he was become a mere Skeleton, and was sick almost to death for some Months afterwards. At last, however, by Dint of Reflection, he got the better of his Distemper; and the Acuteness of the Pain he underwent, in some Measure, contributed towards his Consolation.

Since I have met with such an unexpected Repulse, said he, from a capricious Court-Lady, I am determin'd to marry some substantial Citizen's Daughter. He pitch'd accordingly upon *Azora*, a young Gentlewoman extremely well- bred, an excellent Oeconomist, and one, whose Parents were very rich.

Their Nuptials accordingly were soon after solemniz'd, and for a whole Month successively, no two Turtles were ever more fond of each other. In Process of Time, however, he perceiv'd she was a little Coquettish, and too much inclin'd to think, that the handsomest young Fellows were always the most virtuous and the greatest Wits.

CHAP. II.

The Nose.

O ne Day *Azora*, as she was just return'd home from taking a short Country airing, threw herself into a violent Passion, and swell'd with Invectives. What, in God's Name, my Dear, said *Zadig*, has thus ruffled your Temper? What can be the Meaning of all these warm Exclamations? Alas! said she, you would have been disgusted as much as I am, had you been an Eyewitness of that Scene of Female Falshood, as I was Yesterday. I went, you must know, to visit the disconsolate Widow *Cosrou*, who has been these
two Days erecting a Monument to the Memory of her young deceased Husband, near the Brook that runs on one side of her Meadow. She made the most solemn Vow, in the Height of her Affliction, never to stir from that Tomb, as long as ever that Rivulet took its usual Course.—Well! and wherein, pray, said *Zadig*, is the good Woman so much to blame? Is it not an incontestable Mark of her superior Merit and Conjugal-Affection? But, *Zadig*, said *Azora*, was you to know how her Thoughts were employ'd when I made my Visit, you'd never forget or forgive her. Pray, my dearest *Azora*, what then was she about? Why, the Creature, said *Azora*, was studying, to be sure, to find out Ways and Means to turn the Current of the River.

Azora, in short, harangu'd so long, and, was so big with her Invectives against the young Widow, that her too affected, vain Shew of Virtue, gave *Zadig* a secret Disgust.

Zadig had an intimate Friend, one *Cador* by Name, whose Spouse was perfectly honest, and had in reality a greater Regard for him, than all Mankind besides: This Friend *Zadig* made his Confident, and bound him to keep a Project of his entirely a Secret, by a Promise of some valuable Token of his Respect. *Azora* had been visiting a Female Companion for two Days together in the Country, and on the third was returning home: No sooner, however, was she in Sight of the House, but the Servants ran to meet her with Tears in their Eyes, and told her, that their Master dy'd suddenly the Night before; that they durstn't carry her the doleful Tidings, but were going to bury *Zadig* in the Sepulchre of his Ancestors, at the Bottom of the Garden. She burst into a Flood of Tears; tore her Hair; and vow'd to die by his Side. As soon as it was dark, young *Cador* came, and begg'd the Favour of being introduc'd to the Widow. He was so, and they wept together very cordially. Next Day the Storm was somewhat abated, and they din'd together; *Cador* inform'd her, that his Friend had left him the much greater Part of his Effects, and gave her to understand, that he should think himself the happiest Creature in the World, if she would condescend to be his Partner in that Demise. The Widow wept, sobb'd, and began to melt. More Time was spent in Supper than at Dinner. They discoursed together with a little more Freedom. *Azora* was lavish of her Encomiums on *Zadig*; but then, 'twas true, she said, he had some secret Infirmities to which *Cador* was a Stranger. In the Midst of their Midnight Entertainment, *Cador* all on a sudden complain'd that he was taken with a most violent pleuretic Fit, and was ready to swoon away. Our Lady being extremely concern'd, and over-officious, flew to her Closet of Cordials, and brought down every Thing she could think of that might be of Service on this emergent Occasion. She was extremely sorry that the famous *Hermes* was gone from *Babylon*, and condescended to lay her warm Hand upon the Part affected, in which he felt such an agonizing Pain. Pray Sir, said she, in a soft, languishing Tone, are you subject to this tormenting Malady? Sometimes, Madam, said *Cador*, so strong, that they bring me almost to Death's Door; and there is but one Thing can infallibly cure me; and that is, the Application of a dead Man's Nose to the part affected. An odd Remedy truly, said *Azora*. Not stranger, Madam, said he, than the Great *Arnon's* * There was at this Time in *Babylon*, a famous Doctor, nam'd *Arnon*, who both cur'd Apoplectic Fits, and prevented them from affecting his Patients, as was frequently advertiz'd in the Gazettes, by a little never-failing Purse that he hung round their Necks. infallible Apoplectic Necklaces.

This Assurance of Success, together with *Cador*'s personal Merit, determin'd *Azora* in his Favour. After all, said she, when my Husband shall be about to cross the Bridge *Tchimavar*, from this World of Yesterday, to the other, of To-morrow, will the Angel *Asrael*, think you, make any Scruple about his Passage, should his Nose prove something shorter in the next Life than 'twas in this? She would venture, however, and taking up a sharp Razor, repair'd to her Husband's Tomb; water'd it first with her Tears, and then intended to perform the innocent Operation, as he lay extended breathless, as she thought, in his Coffin. *Zadig* mounted in a Moment; secur'd his Nose with one Hand, and the Incision-Knife with the other. Madam, said he, never more exclaim against the Widow *Cosrou*. The Scheme for cutting my Nose off was much closer laid than hers of throwing the River into a new Channel.

CHAP. III.

The Dog *and the* Horse.

Z *adig* found, by Experience, that the first thirty Days of Matrimony (as 'tis written in the Book of *Zend*) is Honey-Moon; but the second is all Wormwood. He was oblig'd, in short, as *Azora* grew such a Termagant, to sue out a Bill of Divorce, and to seek his Consolation for the future, in the Study of Nature. Who is happier, said he, than the Philosopher, who peruses with Understanding that spacious Book, which the supreme Being has laid open before his Eyes? The Truths he discovers there, are of infinite Service to him. He thereby cultivates and improves his Mind. He lives in Peace and Tranquility all his Days; he is afraid of Nobody, and he has no tender, indulgent Wife to shorten his Nose for him.

Wrapped up in these Contemplations, he retir'd to a little Country House on the Banks of the *Euphrates*; there he never spent his Time in calculating how many Inches of Water run thro' the Arch of a Bridge in a second of Time, or in enquiring if a Cube Line of Rain falls more in the *Mouse-Month*, than in that of the *Ram*. He form'd no Projects for making Silk Gloves and Stockings out of Spiders Webbs, nor of China-Ware out of broken Glass-Bottles; but he pry'd into the Nature and Properties of Animals and Plants, and soon, by his strict and repeated Enquiries, he was capable of discerning a Thousand Variations in visible Objects, that others, less curious, imagin'd were all alike.

One Day, as he was taking a solitary Walk by the Side of a Thicket, he espy'd one of the Queen's Eunuchs, with several of his Attendants, coming towards him, hunting about, in deep Concern, both here and there, like Persons almost in Despair, and seeking, with Impatience, for something lost of the utmost Importance. Young Man, said the Queen's chief Eunuch, have not you seen, pray, her Majesty's Dog? *Zadig* very cooly replied, you mean her Bitch, I presume. You say very right Sir, said the Eunuch, 'tis a Spaniel-Bitch indeed. —And very small said *Zadig*: She has had Puppies too lately; she's a little lame with her left Fore-foot, and has long Ears. By your exact Description, Sir, you must doubtless have seen her, said the Eunuch, almost out of Breath. But I have not Sir, notwithstanding, neither did I know, but by you, that the Queen ever had such a favourite Bitch.

Just at this critical Juncture, so various are the Turns of Fortune's Wheel! the best Palfrey in all the King's Stable had broke loose from the Groom, and got upon the Plains of *Babylon*. The Head Huntsman with all his inferior Officers, were in Pursuit after him, with as much Concern, as the Eunuch about the

Bitch. The Head Huntsman address'd himself to *Zadig*, and ask'd him, whether he hadn't seen the King's Palfrey run by him. No Horse, said *Zadig*, ever gallop'd smoother; he is about five Foot high, his Hoofs are very small; his Tail is about three Foot six Inches long; the studs of his Bit are of pure Gold, about 23 Carats; and his Shoes are of Silver, about Eleven penny Weight a-piece. What Course did he take, pray, Sir? Whereabouts is he, said the Huntsman? I never sat Eyes on him, reply'd *Zadig*, not I, neither did I ever hear before now, that his Majesty had such a Palfrey.

The Head Huntsman, as well as the Head Eunuch, upon his answering their Interrogatories so very exactly, not doubting in the least, but that *Zadig* had clandestinely convey'd both the Bitch and the Horse away, secur'd him, and carried him before the grand Desterham, who condemn'd him to the *Knout*, and to be confin'd for Life in some remote and lonely Part of *Siberia*. No sooner had the Sentence been pronounc'd, but the Horse and Bitch were both found. The Judges were in some Perplexity in this odd Affair, and yet thought it absolutely necessary, as the Man was innocent, to recal their Decree. However, they laid a Fine upon him of Four Hundred Ounces of Gold, for his false Declaration of his not having seen, what doubtless he did: And the Fine was order'd to be deposited in Court accordingly: On the Payment whereof, he was permitted to bring his Cause on to a Hearing before the grand Desterham.

On the Day appointed for that Purpose he open'd the Cause himself, in Terms to this or the like Effect.

Ye bright Stars of Justice, ye profound Abyss of universal Knowledge, ye Mirrors of Equity, who have in you the Solidity of Lead, the Hardness of Steel, the Lustre of a Diamond, and the Resemblance of the purest Gold! Since ye have condescended so far, as to admit of my Address to this August Assembly, I here, in the most solemn Manner, swear to you by *Orosmades*, that I never saw the Queen's illustrious Bitch, nor the sacred Palfrey of the King of Kings. I'll be ingenuous, however, and declare the Truth, and nothing but the Truth. As I was walking by the Thicket's Side, where I met with her Majesty's most venerable chief Eunuch, and the King's most illustrious chief Huntsman, I perceiv'd upon the Sand the Footsteps of an Animal, and I easily inferr'd that it must be a little one. The several small, tho' long Ridges of Land between the Footsteps of the Creature, gave me just Grounds to imagine it was a Bitch whose Teats hung down; and for that Reason, I concluded she had but lately pupp'd. As I observ'd likewise some other Traces, in some Degree different, which seem'd to have graz'd all the Way upon the Surface of the Sand, on the Side of the fore-Feet, I knew well enough she must have had long Ears. And forasmuch as I discern'd; with some Degree of Curiosity, that the Sand was every where less hollow'd by one Foot in particular, than by the other three, I conceiv'd that the Bitch of our most august Queen was somewhat lamish, if I may presume to say so.

As to the Palfrey of the King of Kings, give me leave to inform you, that as I was walking down the Lane by the Thicket-side, I took particular Notice of the Prints made upon the Sand by a Horse's Shoes; and found that their Distances were in exact Proportion; from that Observation, I concluded the Palfrey gallop'd well. In the next Place, the Dust of some Trees in a narrow Lane, which was but seven Foot broad, was here and there swept off, both on the Right and on the Left, about three Feet and six Inches from the Middle of the Road. For which Reason I pronounc'd the Tail of the Palfrey to be three Foot and a half long, with which he had whisk'd off the Dust on both Sides as he ran along. Again, I perceiv'd under the Trees, which form'd a Kind of Bower of five Feet high, some Leaves that had been lately fallen on the Ground, and I was sensible the Horse must have shook them off; from whence I conjectur'd he was five Foot high. As to the Bits of his Bridle, I knew they must be of Gold, and of the Value I mention'd; for he had rubb'd the Studs upon a certain Stone, which I knew to be a Touch-stone, by an Experiment that I had made of it. To conclude, by the Prints which his Shoes had left of some Flint-Stones of another Nature, I concluded his Shoes were Silver, and of eleven penny Weight Fineness, as I before mention'd.

The whole Bench of Judges stood astonish'd at the Profundity of *Zadig*'s nice Discernment. The News was soon carried to the King and the Queen. *Zadig* was not only the whole Subject of the Court's Conversation; but his Name was mention'd with the utmost Veneration in the King's Chambers, and his Privy-Council. And notwithstanding several of their Magi declar'd he ought to be burnt for a Sorcerer; yet the King thought proper, that the Fine he had deposited in Court, should be peremptorily restor'd. The Clerk of the Court, the Tipstaffs, and other petty Officers, waited on him in their proper Habit, in order to refund the four Hundred Ounces of Gold, pursuant to the King's express Order; modestly reserving only three Hundred and ninety Ounces, part thereof, to defray the Fees of the Court. And the Domesticks swarm'd about him likewise, in Hopes of some small Consideration.

Zadig, upon winding up of the Bottom, was fully convinc'd, that it was very dangerous to be over-wise; and was determin'd to set a Watch before the Door of his Lips for the future.

An Opportunity soon offer'd for the Trial of his Resolution. A Prisoner of State had just made his Escape, and pass'd under the Window of *Zadig*'s House. *Zadig* was examin'd thereupon, but was absolutely dumb. However, as it was plainly prov'd upon him, that he did look out of the Window at the same Time, he was sentenc'd to pay five Hundred Ounces of Gold for that Misdemeanor; and moreover, was oblig'd to thank the Court for their Indulgence; a Compliment which the Magistrates of *Babylon* expect to be paid them. Good God! said he, to himself, have I not substantial Reason to complain, that my impropitious Stars should direct me to walk by a Wood's-Side, where the Queen's Bitch and the King's Palfrey should happen to pass by? How dangerous is it to pop one's Head out of one's Window? And, in a Word, how difficult is it for a Man to be happy on this Side the Grave?

CHAP. IV.

The ENVIOUS MAN.

A s *Zadig* had met with such a Series of Misfortunes, he was determin'd to ease the Weight of them by the Study of Philosophy, and the Conversation of select Friends. He was still possess'd of a little pretty Box in the Out-parts of *Babylon*, which was furnish'd in a good Taste; where every Artist was welcome, and wherein he enjoy'd all the rational Pleasures that a virtuous Man could well wish for. In the Morning, his Library was always open for the Use of the Learned; at Night his Table was fill'd with the most agreeable Companions; but he was soon sensible, by Experience, how dangerous it was to keep learned Men Company. A warm Dispute arose about a certain Law of *Zoroaster*; which prohibited the Eating of Griffins: But to what Purpose said some of the Company, was that Prohibition, since there is no such Animal in Nature? Some again insisted that there must; for otherwise *Zoroaster* could never have been so weak as to give his Pupils such a Caution. *Zadig*, in order to compromize the Matter, said; Gentlemen, If there are such Creatures in Being, let us never touch them; and if there are not, we are well assur'd we can't touch them; so in either Case we shall comply with the Commandment.

A learned Man at the upper End of the Table, who had compos'd thirteen Volumes, expatiating on every Property of the Griffin, took this Affair in a very serious Light, which would greatly have embarrass'd *Zadig*, but for the Credit of a Magus, who was Brother to his Friend *Cador*. From that Day forward, *Zadig* ever distinguish'd and preferr'd good, before learned Company: He associated with the most conversible Men, and the most amiable Ladies in all *Babylon*; he made elegant Entertainments, which were frequently preceded by a Concert of Musick, and enliven'd by the most facetious Conversation, in which, as he had felt the Smart of it, he had laid aside all Thoughts of shewing his Wit, which is not only the surest Proof that a Man has none, but the most infallible Means to spoil all good Company.

Neither the Choice of his Friends, nor that of his Dishes, was the Result of Pride or Ostentation. He took Delight in appearing to be, what he actually was, and not in seeming to be what he was not; and by that Means, got a greater real Character than he actually aim'd at.

Directly opposite to his House liv'd *Arimazes*, one puff'd up with Pride, who not meeting with Success in the World, sought his Revenge in railing against all Mankind. Rich as he was, it was almost more than he could accomplish, to procure ev'n any Parasites about him. Tho' the rattling of the Chariots which stopp'd at *Zadig*'s Door was a perfect Nuisance to him; yet the good Character which every Body gave him was still a higher Provocation. He would sometimes intrude himself upon *Zadig*, and set down at his Table without any Invitation; when there, he would most certainly interrupt the Mirth of the Company, as Harpies, they say, infect the very Carrion that they eat.

Arimazes took it in his Head one Day to invite a young Lady to an Entertainment; but she, instead of accepting of his Offer, spent the Evening at *Zadig*'s. Another Time, as *Zadig* and he were chatting together at Court, a Minister of State came up to them, and invited *Zadig* to Supper, but took no Notice of *Arimazes*. The most implacable Aversions have frequently no better Foundations. This Gentleman, who was call'd the *envious Man*, would have taken away the Life of *Zadig* if he could because most People distinguish'd him by the Title of the *Happy Man*. "An Opportunity of doing Mischief, says *Zoroaster*, offers itself a hundred Times a Day; but that of doing a Friend a good Office but once a Year."

Arimazes went one Day to *Zadig*'s House, when he was walking in his Garden with two Friends, and a young Lady, to whom he said Abundance of fine Things, with no other Design but the innocent Pleasure of saying them. Their Conversation turn'd on a War that the King had happily put an End to, between him and his Vassal, the Prince of *Hyrcania*. *Zadig* having signaliz'd himself in that short War, commended his Majesty very highly, but was more lavish of his Compliments on the Lady. He took out his Pocket Book, and wrote four extempore Verses on that Occasion, and gave them the Lady to read. The Gentlemen then present begg'd to be oblig'd with a Sight of them, as well as the Lady, But either thro' Modesty, or rather a self-Consciousness that he hadn't happily succeeded, he gave them a flat Denial. He was sensible, that a sudden poetic Flight must prove insipid to every one but the Person in whose Favour it is written, whereupon he snapt the Table in two whereon the Lines were wrote, and threw both Pieces into a Rose-bush, where they were hunted for, but to no Purpose. Soon after it happened to rain, and all the Company flew into the House, but *Arimazes*. Notwithstanding the Shower, he continued in the Garden, and never quitted it, till he had found one Moiety of the Tablet, which was unfortunately broke in such a Manner, that even the half Lines were good sense, and good Metre, tho' very short. But what was still more remarkably unfortunate, they appear'd at first View, to be a severe satyr upon the King: The Words were these:

> *To flagrant Crimes*
>
> *His Crown he owes;*
>
> *To peaceful Times*
>
> *The worst of Foes.*

This was the first Moment that ever *Arimazes* was happy. He had it now in his Power to ruin the most virtuous and innocent of Men. Big with his execrable Joy, he flew to his Majesty with this virulent Satyr of *Zadig*'s under his own Hand. Not only *Zadig*, but his two Friends and the Lady were immediately close confin'd. His Cause was soon over; for the Judges turn'd a deaf Ear to what he had to say. When Sentence of Condemnation was pass'd upon him, *Arimazes*, still spiteful, was heard to say, as he went out of Court, with an Air of Contempt, that *Zadig*'s Lines were Treason indeed, but nothing more. Tho' *Zadig* didn't value himself on Account of his Genius for Poetry; yet he was almost distracted to find himself condemn'd for the worst of Traitors, and his two Friends and the Lady lock'd up in a Dungeon for a Crime, of which he was no ways guilty. He wasn't permitted to speak one Word for himself. His Pocket-Book was sufficient Evidence against him. So strict were the Laws of *Babylon*! He was carried to the Place of Execution, through a Croud of Spectators, who durstn't condole with him, and who flock'd about him, to observe whether his Countenance chang'd, or whether he died with a good Grace. His Relations were the only real Mourners; for there was no Estate in Reversion for them; three Parts of his Effects were confiscated for the King's Use, and the fourth was devoted, as a Reward, to the use of the Informer.

Just at the Time that he was preparing himself for Death, the King's Parrot flew from her Balcony, into *Zadig*'s Garden, and alighted on a Rose-bush. A Peach, that had been blown down, and drove by the Wind from an adjacent Tree, just under the Bush, was glew'd, as it were, to the other Moiety of the Tablet. Away flew the Parrot with her Booty, and return'd to the King's Lap. The Monarch, being somewhat curious, read the Words on the broken Tablet, which had no Meaning in them as he could perceive, but seem'd to be the broken Parts of a Tetrastick. He was a great Admirer of Poetry; and the odd Adventure of his Parrot, put him upon Reflection. The Queen who recollected full well the Lines that were wrote on the Fragment of *Zadig*'s Tablet, order'd that Part of it to be produc'd: Both the broken Pieces being put together, they answered exactly the Indentures; and then the Verses which *Zadig* had written, in a Flight of Loyalty, ran thus,

> *Tyrants are prone to flagrant Crimes;*
>
> *To Clemency his Crown he owes;*

To Concord and to peaceful Times,

Love only is the worst of Foes.

Upon this the King order'd *Zadig* to be instantly brought before him; and his two Friends and the Lady to be that Moment discharg'd. *Zadig*, as he stood before the King and Queen, fix'd his Eyes upon the Ground, and begg'd their Majesty's Pardon for his little worthless, poetical Attempt. He spoke, however, with such a becoming Grace, and with so much Modesty and good Sense, that the King and the Queen, ordered him to be brought before them once again. He was brought accordingly, and he pleas'd them still more and more. In short, they gave him all the immense Estate of *Arimazes*, who had so unjustly accus'd him; but *Zadig* generously return'd the wicked Informer the Whole to a Farthing. The envious Man, however, was no ways affected, but with the Restoration of his Effects. *Zadig* every Day grew more and more in Favour at Court. He was made a Party in all the King's Pleasures, and nothing was done in the Privy-Council without him. The Queen, from that very Hour, shew'd him so much Respect, and spoke to him in such soft and endearing Terms, that in Process of Time, it prov'd of fatal Consequence to herself, her Royal Consort, to *Zadig*, and the whole Kingdom. *Zadig* now began to think it was not so difficult a Thing to be happy as at first he imagin'd.

CHAP. V.

The Force *of* Generosity.

T he Time now drew near for the Celebration of a grand Festival, which was kept but once in five Years. 'Twas a constant Custom in *Babylon* at the Expiration of the Term above-mention'd, to distinguish that Citizen from all the Rest, in the most solemn Manner, who had done the most generous Action; and the Grandees and Magi always sat as Judges. The *Satrap* inform'd them of every praise-worthy Deed that occurr'd within his District. All were put to the Vote, and the King himself pronounc'd the Definitive
Sentence. People of all Ranks and Degrees came from the remotest Part of the Kingdom to be present at this Solemnity. The Victor, whoever he was, receiv'd from the King's own Hand a golden Cup, enrich'd with precious Stones, and upon the Delivery, the King made use of the following Salutation. *Receive this Reward of your Generosity, and may the Gods grant me Thousands of such valuable Subjects!*

Upon this memorable Day, the King appear'd in all the Pomp imaginable on his Throne of State, surrounded by his Grandees, the Magi, and the Deputies, from all the surrounding Nations, of every Province that attended these public Sports, where Honour was to be acquir'd, not by the Velocity of the best Race-Horse, or by bodily Strength, but by intrinsic Merit. The principal *Satrap* proclaim'd, with an audible Voice, such Actions as would entitle the Victor to the inestimable Prize; but never mention'd one Word of *Zadig*'s Greatness of Soul, in returning his invidious Neighbour all his Estate, notwithstanding he would have taken away his Life: That was but a Trifle, and not worth speaking of.

The first that was set up for the Prize, was a Judge, that had occasion'd a Citizen to lose a very considerable Cause, through some Mistake, for which he was no ways responsible, and made him Restitution out of his private Purse.

The next Candidate was a Youth, that tho' violently in Love with one that he intended shortly to make his Spouse, yet resign'd her to his Friend, who was just expiring at her Feet; and moreover, gave her a Portion at the same Time.

After this appear'd a Soldier, who, in the *Hyrcanian* War, had done a much more glorious Action than the Lover. A Gang of *Hyrcanians* having taken his Mistress from him, he fought them bravely, and rescued her out of their Hands: Soon after, he was inform'd, that another Band of the same Party had hurried away his Mother to a Place not far distant; he left his Mistress, all drown'd in Tears, and ran to his Mother's Assistance: After that Skirmish was over, he returned to his Sweet-heart, and found her just expiring. He would fain have plung'd a Dagger into his Heart that Moment; but his Mother remonstrated to him, that, should he die, she should be entirely helpless, and upon that Account only he had Courage to live a little longer.

The Judges seem'd very much inclin'd to give their Votes for the Soldier; but the King prevented them, by saying, that the Soldier's Action was praiseworthy enough, and so were those of the rest, but none of them give me any Surprize. What *Zadig* did Yesterday perfectly struck me with Astonishment. I'll mention another Instance. I had some few Days ago, as a Testimony of my Resentment, banish'd my Prime-Minister, and Favourite *Coreb* from the Court. I complain'd of his Conduct in the warmest Terms; and all my Sycophants about me, told me that I was too merciful; and loaded him with the sharpest Invectives. I ask'd *Zadig* what his Opinion was of *Coreb*; and he dar'd to give him the best of Characters. I must confess, I have read in our publick Records, indeed, of Instances where Restitution have been generally made, for Injuries committed by Mistake; where a Mistress has been resign'd; and where a Mother has been preferr'd to a Mistress; but I never read of a Courtier, that would speak to the Advantage of a Minister in Disgrace, and against whom the Sovereign was highly incens'd. I'll give 20,000 Pieces of Gold to every Candidate that has been this Day proclaim'd, but I'll give the Cup to no one but *Zadig*.

Sire, said *Zadig*, 'tis your Majesty alone, that deserves the Cup; 'tis you alone who have done an Action of Generosity, never heard of before; since you, who are King of Kings, wasn't exasperated against your Slave, when he contradicted you in the Heat of your Passion. Every Body gaz'd with Eyes of Admiration on the King and *Zadig*. The Judge, who had generously made Restitution for his Error; the Lover, who had married his Mistress to his Friend; the Soldier, who had preferr'd the Welfare of his Mother to that of his Mistress; received the promis'd Donation from the Monarch, and saw their Names register'd in the Book of *Fame*: But *Zadig* had the Cup. The King got the universal Character of a good Prince, which he did not long preserve. This joyful Day was solemniz'd with Festivals beyond the Time by Law establish'd. Tragedies were acted there that drew Tears from the Spectators; and Comedies that made them laugh; Entertainments, that the *Babylonians* were perfect Strangers to: The Commemoration of it is still preserv'd in *Asia*. Now, said *Zadig*, I am happy at last; but he was grosly mistaken.

CHAP. VI.

The JUDGMENTS.

Y oung as *Zadig* was, he was constituted chief Judge of all the Tribunals throughout the Empire. He fill'd the Place, like one, whom the Gods had endow'd with the strictest Justice, and the most solid Wisdom. It was to him, the Nations round about were indebted for that generous Maxim; *that 'tis much more Prudence to acquit two Persons, tho' actually guilty, than to pass Sentence of Condemnation in one that is virtuous and innocent.* It was his firm Opinion, that the Laws were intended to be a Praise to those who did well, as much as to be a Terror to Evildoers. It was his peculiar Talent to render Truth as obvious as possible: Whereas most Men study to render it intricate and obscure. On the very first Day of his Entrance into his High Office, he exerted this peculiar Talent. A rich Merchant, and a Native of *Babylon*, died in the *Indies*. He had made his Will, and appointed his two Sons Joint-Heirs of his Estate, as soon as they had settled their Sister, and married her with their mutual Approbation. Moreover, he left a specific Legacy of 30,000 Pieces of Gold to that Son, who should, after his Decease, be prov'd to love him best. The Eldest erected to his Memory a very costly Monument: The Youngest appropriated a considerable Part of his Bequest to the Augmentation of his Sister's Fortune: Every one, without Hesitation, gave the Preference to the Elder, allowing the Younger to have the greatest Affection for his Sister. The Legacy therefore was doubtless due to the Eldest.

Their Cause came before *Zadig*, and he examin'd them apart. To the former, said *Zadig*, Your Father, Sir, is not dead, as is reported, but being happily recover'd, is on his Return to *Babylon*. God be praised, said the young Man! but I hope the Expence I have been at in raising this superb Monument will be consider'd. After this, *Zadig* repeated the same Story to the Younger. God be praised, said he! I will immediately restore all that he has left me; but I hope my Father will not recal the little Present I have made my Sister. You have nothing to restore, Sir; you shall have the Legacy of the thirty thousand Pieces; for 'tis you that have the greatest Veneration for your deceased Father.

A young Lady that was very rich, had entred into a Marriage-Contract with two *Magis*; and having receiv'd Instructions from both Parties for some Months, she prov'd with Child. They were both ready and willing to marry her. But, said she, he shall be my Husband, that has put me into a Capacity of serving my Country, by adding one to it. 'Tis I, Madam, that have answered that valuable End, said one; but the other insisted 'twas his Operation. Well! said she, since this is a Moot-point, I'll acknowledge him for the Father of the

Child, that will give him the most liberal Education. In a short Time after, my Lady was brought to Bed of a hopeful Boy. Each of them insisted on being Tutor, and the Cause was brought before *Zadig*. The two Magi were order'd to appear in Court. Pray Sir, said *Zadig* to the first, what Method of Instruction do you propose to pursue for the Improvement of your young Pupil? He shall first be grounded, said this learned Pedagogue, in the Eight Parts of Speech; then I'll teach him Logic, Astrology, Magick, the wide Difference between the Terms Substance and Accident, Abstract and Concrete, &c. &c. As for my Part, Sir, I shall take another Course, said the second; I'll do my utmost to make him an honest Man, and acceptable to his Friends. Upon this, *Zadig* said, you, Sir, shall marry the Mother, let who will be the Father.

There came daily Complaints to Court against the *Itimadoulet* of *Media*, whose Name was *Irax*. He was a Person of Quality, who was possess'd of a very considerable Estate, notwithstanding he had squander'd away a great Part of it, by indulging himself in all Manner of expensive Pleasures. It was but seldom that an Inferior was suffer'd to speak to him; but not a Soul durst contradict him: No Peacock was more gay; no Turtle more amorous; and no Tortoise more indolent and inactive. He made false Glory and false Pleasures his sole Pursuit.

Zadig, undertaking to cure him, sent him forthwith, as by express Order from the King, a Musick-Master with twelve Voices, and 24 Violins, as his Attendants; a Head Steward, with six Men Cooks, and 4 Chamberlains, who were never to be out of his Sight. The King issued out his Writ for the punctual Observance of his Royal Will; and thus the Affair proceeded.

The first Morning, as soon as the voluptuous *Irax* had open'd his Eyes, his Musick-Master, with the Voices and Violins, entred his Apartment. They sang a Cantata, that lasted two Hours and three Minutes. Every three Minutes the Chorus, or Burthen of the Song, was to this Effect.

Tisn't in Words to speak your Praise;

What mighty Honours are your Due!

To worth like yours we Altars raise,

No Monarch's happier, Sir, than you.

After the Cantata was over, the Chamberlain address'd him in a formal Harangue for three Quarters of an Hour without ceasing; wherein he took Occasion to extol every Virtue to which he was a perfect Stranger; when the Oration was over, he was conducted to Dinner, where the Musicians were all in waiting, and play'd, as soon as he was seated at his Table. Dinner lasted three Hours before he condescended to speak a Word. When he did; you say Right, Sir, said the chief Chamberlain; scarce had he utter'd four Words more, but Right, Sir, said the second. The other two Chamberlain's Time was taken up in laughing with Admiration at *Irax*'s Smart Repartees, or at least such as he ought to have made. After the Cloth was taken away, the adulating Chorus was repeated.

This first Day *Irax* was all in Raptures; he imagin'd, that this Honour done him by the King of Kings, was the sole Result of his exalted Merit. The second wasn't altogether so agreeable; The third prov'd somewhat troublesome; the fourth insupportable; the fifth was tormenting; and at last, he was perfectly outrageous at the continual Peal in his Ears of No Monarch's happier Sir, than you, You say right, *&c.* and at being daily harangu'd at the same Hour. Whereupon he wrote to Court, and begg'd of his Majesty to recal his Chamberlain, his Musick-Master, and all his Retinue, his Head Steward and his Cooks, and promis'd, in the most submissive Manner, to be less vain, and more industrious for the future. Tho' he didn't require so much Adulations, nor such grand Entertainments, he was much more happy; for, as *Sadder* has it, *One continued Scene of Pleasure, is no Pleasure at all.*

Zadig every Day gave incontestable Proofs of his wondrous Penetration, and the Goodness of his Heart; he was ador'd by the People, and was the Darling of the King. The little Difficulties that he met with in the first Stage of his Life, serv'd only to augment his present Felicity. Every Night, however, he had some unlucky Dream or another, that gave him some Disturbance. One while, he imagin'd himself extended on a Bed of wither'd Plants, amongst which there were some that were sharp pointed, and made him very restless and uneasy; another Time, he fancied himself repos'd on a Bed of Roses, out of which rush'd a Serpent, that stung him to the Heart with his envenom'd Tongue. Alas! said he, waking, I was one while upon a Bed of hard and nauseous Plants, and just this Moment repos'd on a Bed of Roses. But then the Serpent.———

CHAP. VII.

The Force of JEALOUSY.

T he Misfortunes that attended *Zadig* proceeded, in a great Measure, from his Preferment; but more from his intrinsic Merit. Every Day he had familiar Converse with the King, his Royal Master, and his august Consort, *Astarte*. And the Pleasure arising from thence was greatly enhanc'd from an innate Ambition of pleasing, which, in regard to Wit, is the same, as Dress is to Beauty. His Youth, and graceful Deportment, had a greater Influence on *Astarte*, than she was at first aware of. Tho' her Affection for him daily encreas'd; yet she was perfectly innocent. *Astarte* would say, without the least Reserve or Apprehension of Fear, that she was extreamly pleas'd with the Company of one, who was, not only a Favourite of her Husband, but the Darling of the whole Empire. She was continually speaking in his Commendation before the King: He was the Subject of her whole Discourse amongst her Ladies of Honour, who were as lavish of their Praises as herself. Such repeated Discourses, however innocent, made a deeper Impression on her Heart, than she at that Time apprehended. She would every now and then send *Zadig* some little Present or another; which he construed as the Result of a greater Value for him than she intended. She said no more of him, as she thought, than a Queen might innocently do, who was perfectly assur'd of his Attachment to her Husband; sometimes, indeed, she would express her self with an Air of Tenderness and Affection.

Astarte was much handsomer than either his Mistress *Semira*, who had such a natural Antipathy to a one-eyed Lord, or *Azora*, his late loving Spouse, that would innocently have cut his Nose off. The Freedoms which *Astarte* took, her tender Expressions, at which she began to blush, the Glances of her Eye, which she would turn away, if perceiv'd, and which she fix'd upon his, kindled in the Heart of *Zadig* a Fire, which struck him with Amazement. He did all he could to smother it; he call'd up all the Philosophy he was Master of to his Aid; but all in vain, for no Consolation arose from those Reflections.

Duty, Gratitude, and an injur'd Monarch, presented themselves before his Eyes, as avenging Deities: He bravely struggled; he triumph'd indeed; but this Conquest over his Passions, which he was oblig'd to check every Moment, cost him many a deep Sigh and Tear. He durst not talk with the Queen any more, with that Freedom which was too engaging on both Sides; his Eyes were obnubilated; his Discourse was forc'd and unconnected; he turn'd his Eyes another Way; and when, against his Inclination, they met with those of the Queen, he found, that tho' drown'd in Tears, they darted Flames of Fire:

They seem'd in Silence to intimate, that they were afraid of being in love with each other; and that both burn'd with a Fire which both condemn'd.

Zadig flew from her Presence, like one beside himself, and in Despair; his Heart was over-charg'd with a Burthen, too great for him to bear: In the Heat of his Conflicts, he disclos'd the Secrets of his Heart to his trusty Friend *Cador*, as one, who, having long groan'd under the Weight of an inexpressible Anguish of Mind, at once makes known the Cause of his Torments by the Groans, as it were, extorted from him, and by the Drops of a cold Sweat, that trickled down his Cheeks.

Cador said to him; 'tis now some considerable Time since, I have discover'd that secret Passion which you have foster'd in your Bosom, and yet endeavour'd to conceal even from your self. The Passions carry along with them such strong Impressions, that they cannot be conceal'd. Tell me ingenuously *Zadig*; and be your own Accuser, whether or no, since I have made this Discovery, the King has not shewn some visible Marks of his Resentment. He has no other Foible, but that of being the most jealous Mortal breathing. You take more Pains to check the Violence of your Passion, than the Queen herself does; because you are a Philosopher; because, in short, you are *Zadig*; *Astarte* is but a weak Woman; and tho' her Eyes speak too visibly, and with too much Imprudence; yet she does not think her self blame-worthy. Being conscious of her Innocence, to her own Misfortune, as well as yours, she is too unguarded. I tremble for her; because I am sensible her Conscience acquits her. Were you both agreed, you might conceal your Regard for each other from all the World: A rising Passion, that is smother'd, breaks out into a Flame; Love, when once gratified, knows how to conceal itself with Art. *Zadig* shudder'd at the Proposition of ungratefully violating the Bed of his Royal Benefactor; and never was there a more loyal Subject to a Prince, tho' guilty of an involuntary Crime. The Queen, however, repeated the Name of *Zadig* so often, and her Cheeks glow'd with such a red, when ever she utter'd it; she was one while so transported, and at another, so dejected, when the Discourse turn'd upon him in the King's Presence; she was in such a Reverie, so confus'd and stupid, when he went out of the Presence, that her Deportment made the King extremely uneasy. He was convinc'd of every Thing he saw, and form'd in his Mind an Idea of a thousand Things he did not see. He observ'd, particularly, that *Astarte*'s Sandals were blue; so *Zadig*'s were blue likewise; that as the Queen wore yellow Ribbands, *Zadig*'s Turbet was of the same Colour: These were shocking Circumstances for a Monarch of his Cast of Mind to reflect on! To a Mind, in short, so distemper'd as his was, Suspicions were converted into real Facts.

All Court Slaves, and Sycophants, are so many Spies on Kings and Queens:

They soon discover'd that *Astarte* was fond, and *Moabdar* jealous. *Arimazius*, his envious Foe, who was as incorrigible as ever; for Flints will never soften; and Creatures, that are by Nature venemous, forever retain their Poison. *Arimazius*, I say, wrote an anonymous Letter to *Moabdar*, the infamous Recourse of sordid Spirits, who are the Objects of universal Contempt; but in this Case, an Affair of the last Importance; because this Letter tallied with the baneful Suggestions that Monarch had conceiv'd. In short, his Thoughts were now wholly bent upon Revenge. He determin'd to poison *Astarte* on a certain Night, and to have *Zadig* strangled by Break of Day. Orders for that Purpose were expressly given to a merciless, inhuman Eunuch, the ready Executioner of his Vengeance. At that critical Conjuncture, there happen'd to be a Dwarf, who was dumb, but not deaf, in the King's Apartment. Nobody regarded him: He was an Eye and Ear-witness of all that pass'd, and yet no more suspected than any irrational Domestic Animal. This little Dwarf had conceiv'd a peculiar Regard for *Astarte* and *Zadig*: He heard, with equal Horror and Surprize, the King's Orders to destroy them both. But how to prevent those Orders from being put into Execution, as the Time was so short, was all his Concern. He could not write, 'tis true, but he had luckily learnt to draw, and take a Likeness. He spent a good Part of the Night in delineating with Crayons, on a Piece of Paper, the imminent Danger that thus attended the Queen. In one Corner, he represented the King highly incens'd, and giving his cruel Eunuch the fatal Orders; in another, a Bowl and a Cord upon a Table; in the Center was the Queen, expiring in the Arms of her Maids of Honour, with *Zadig* strangled, and laid dead at her Feet. In the Horizon was the rising Sun, to denote, that this execrable Scene was to be exhibited by Break of Day. No sooner was his Design finish'd, but he ran with it to one of *Astarte*'s Female Favourites, then in waiting, call'd her up, and gave her to understand, that she must carry the Draught to *Astarte* that very Moment.

In the mean Time, the Queen's Attendants, tho' it was Dead of Night, knock'd at the Door of *Zadig*'s Apartment, wak'd him, and deliver'd into his Hands a Billet from the Queen. At first he could not well tell whether he was only in a Dream or not, but soon read the Letter, with a trembling Hand, and a heavy Heart: Words can't express his Surprise, and the Agonies of Despair which he was in upon his perusal of the Contents. *Fly*, said she, *Dear* Zadig, *this very Moment; for your Life's in the utmost Danger: Fly, Dear* Zadig, *I conjure you, in the Name of that fatal Passion, with which I have long struggled, and which I now venture to discover, as I am to make Atonement for it, in a few Moments, by the Loss of my Life. Tho' I am conscious to myself of my Innocence, I find I am to feel the Weight of my Husband's Resentment, and die the Death of a Traitor.*

Zadig was scarce able to speak. He order'd his Friend *Cador* to be instantly call'd, and gave him the Letter the Moment he came, without opening his Lips. *Cador* press'd him to regard the Contents, and to make the best of his Way to *Memphis*. If you presume, said he, to have an Interview with her Majesty first, you inevitably hasten her Execution; or if you wait upon the King, the fatal Consequence will be the same: I'll prevent her unhappy Fate, if possible; you follow but your own: I'll give it out, that you are gone to the *Indies*: I'll wait on you as soon as the Hurricane is blown over, and I'll let you know all that occurs material in *Babylon*.

Cador, that Instant, order'd two of the fleetest Dromedaries that could be got, to be in readiness at a private Back-Door belonging to the Court; he help'd *Zadig* to mount his Beast, tho' ready to drop into the Earth. He had but one trusty Servant to attend him, and *Cador*, overwhelm'd with Grief, soon lost Sight of his dearly beloved Friend.

This illustrious Fugitive soon reach'd the Summit of a little Hill, that afforded him a fair Prospect of the whole City of *Babylon*: But turning his Eyes back towards the Queen's Palace, he fainted away; and when he had recover'd his Senses, he drown'd his Eyes in a Flood of Tears, and with Impatience wish'd for Death. To conclude, after he had reflected, with Horror, on the deplorable Fate of the most amiable Creature in the Universe, and of the most meritorious Queen that ever liv'd; he for a Moment commanded his Passion, and with a Sigh, made the following Exclamations: What is this mortal Life! O Virtue, Virtue, of what Service hast thou been to me! Two young Ladies, a Mistress, and a Wife, have prov'd false to me; a third, who is perfectly innocent, and ten thousand Times handsomer than either of them, has suffer'd Death, 'tis probable, before this, on my Account! All the Acts of Benevolence which I have shewn, have been the Foundation of my Sorrows, and I have been only rais'd to the highest Spoke of Fortune's Wheel, for no other Purpose than to be tumbled down with the greater Force. Had I been as abandon'd as some Miscreants are, I had like them been happy. His Head thus overwhelm'd with these melancholy Reflections, his Eyes thus sunk in his Head, and his meagre Cheeks all pale and languid; and, in a Word, his very Soul thus plung'd in the Abyss of deep Despair, he pursu'd his Journey towards *Egypt*.

CHAP. VIII.

The Thrash'd W<small>IFE</small>.

Z*adig* steer'd his Course by the Stars that shone over his Head. The Constellation of Orion, and the radiant Dog-star directed him towards the Pole of Canope. He reflected with Admiration on those immense Globes of Light, which appear'd to the naked Eye no more than little twinkling Lights; whereas the Earth he was then traversing, which, in Reality, is no more than an imperceptible Point in Nature, seem'd, according to the selfish Idea we generally entertain of it, something very immense, and very magnificent. He then reflected on the whole Race of Mankind, and look'd upon them, as they are in Fact, a Parcel of Insects, or Reptiles, devouring one another on a small Atom of Clay. This just Idea of them greatly alleviated his Misfortunes, recollecting the Nothingness, if we may be allow'd the Expression, of his own Being, and even of *Babylon* itself. His capacious Soul now soar'd into Infinity, and he contemplated, with the same Freedom, as if she was disencumber'd from her earthly Partner, on the immutable Order of the Universe. But as soon as she cower'd her Wings, and resumed her native Seat, he began to consider that *Astarte* might possibly have lost her Life for his Sake; upon which, his Thoughts of the Universe vanish'd all at once, and no other Objects appear'd before his distemper'd Eyes, but his *Astarte* giving up the Ghost, and himself overwhelm'd with a Sea of Troubles: As he gave himself up to this Flux and Reflux of sublime Philosophy and Anxiety of Mind, he was insensibly arriv'd on the Frontiers of *Egypt*: And his trusty Attendant had, unknown to him, stept into the first Village, and sought out for a proper Apartment for his Master and himself. *Zadig* in the mean Time made the best of his Way to the adjacent Gardens; where he saw, not far distant from the High-way, a young Lady, all drown'd in Tears, calling upon Heaven and Earth for Succour in her Distress, and a Man, fir'd with Rage and Resentment, in pursuit after her. He had now just overtaken her, and she fell prostrate at his Feet imploring his Forgiveness. He loaded her with a thousand Reproaches; nor did he spare to chastise her in the most outrageous Manner. By the *Egyptian*'s cruel Deportment towards her, he concluded that the Man was a jealous Husband, and that the Lady was an Inconstant, and had defil'd his Bed: But when he reflected, that the Woman was a perfect Beauty, and to his thinking something like the unfortunate *Astarte*, he perceiv'd his Heart yearn with Compassion towards the Lady, and swell with Indignation against her Tyrant. For Heaven's sake, Sir, assist me, said she, to *Zadig*, sobbing as if her Heart would break, Oh! deliver me out of the Hands of this *Barbarian*:

Save, Sir, O save my Life. Upon these her shocking Outcries, *Zadig* threw himself between the injur'd Lady and the inexorable Brute. And as he had some smattering of the *Egyptian* Tongue, he expostulated with him in his own Dialect, and said: Dear Sir, if you are endow'd with the least Spark of Humanity, let me conjure you to have some Pity and Remorse for so beautiful a Creature; have some Regard, Sir, to the Weakness of her Sex. How can you treat a Lady, who is one of Nature's Master-pieces, in such a rude and outrageous Manner, one who lies weeping at your Feet for Forgiveness, and one who has no other Recourse than her Tears for her Defence? Oh! Oh! said the jealous-pated Fellow in a Fury to *Zadig*, What! You are one of her Gallants, I suppose. I'll be reveng'd of thee, thou Villain, this Moment. No sooner were the Words out of his Mouth, but he quits hold of the Lady, in whose Hair he had twisted his Fingers before, takes up his Lance in a Fury, and endeavours to the utmost of his Pow'r to plunge it in the Stranger's Heart: *Zadig*, however, being cool, warded the intended Blow with Ease. He laid fast hold of his Lance towards the Point. One strove to recover it, and the other to snatch it away by Force. They broke it between them. Whereupon the *Egyptian* drew his Sword. *Zadig* drew his: They fought: The former made a hundred rash Passes one after another, which the latter parried with the utmost Dexterity. The Lady sat herself upon a Grass-plat, adjusting her Head-dress, and looking on the Combatants. The *Egyptian* was too strong for *Zadig*, but *Zadig* was more nimble and active. The latter fought as a Man whose Hand was guided by his Head; the former as a Mad-man who dealt about his Blows at random. *Zadig* took the Advantage, made a Plunge at him, and disarm'd him. And forasmuch as he found that the *Egyptian* was hotter than ever, and endeavour'd all he could to throw him down by Dint of Strength, *Zadig* laid fast hold of him, flew upon him, and tripp'd up his Heels: After that, holding the Point of his Sword to his Breast, like a Man of Honour, gave him his Life. The *Egyptian*, fir'd with Rage, and having no Command of his Passion, drew his Dagger, and wounded *Zadig* like a Coward, whilst the Victor generously forgave him. Upon that unexpected Action, *Zadig*, being incens'd to the last Degree, plung'd his Sword deep into his Bosom. The *Egyptian* fetch'd a hideous Groan, and died upon the Spot. *Zadig* then approach'd the Lady, and with a kind of Concern, in the softest Terms told her, that he was oblig'd to kill her Insulter, tho' against his Inclinations. I have aveng'd your Cause, and deliver'd you out of the merciless Hands of the most outrageous Man I ever saw. Now, Madam, let me know your farther Will and Pleasure with me. You shall die, you Villain! You have murder'd my Love. Oh! I could tear your Heart out. Indeed, Madam, said *Zadig*, you had one of the most hot-headed, oddest Lovers I ever saw. He beat you most unmercifully, and would have taken away my Life because you call'd me in to your Assistance. Would to God he was but alive to beat me again, said she, blubbering and roaring; I

31

deserv'd to be beat. I gave him too just Occasion to be jealous of me. Would to God that he had beat me, and you had died in his Stead! *Zadig* more astonish'd, and more exasperated than ever he was in all his Life, said to her: Really, Madam, you put on such extravagant Airs, that you tempt me, pretty as you are, to thresh you most cordially in my Turn; but I scorn to concern my self any more about you. Upon this, he remounted his Dromedary, and made the best of his Way towards the Village: But before he had got near a hundred Yards, he return'd upon an Out-cry that was made by four Couriers from *Babylon*. They rode full Speed. One of them, spying the young Widow, cried out. There she is, That's she. She answers in every Respect to the Description we had of her. They never took the least Notice of her dead Gallant, but secur'd her directly. Oh! Sir, cried she to *Zadig*, again and again, dear Sir, most generous Stranger, once more deliver me from a Pack of Villains. I most humbly beg your Pardon for my late Conduct and unjust Complaint of you. Do but stand my Friend, at this critical Conjuncture, and I'll be your most obedient Vassal till Death. *Zadig* had now no Inclination to fight for one so undeserving any more. Find some other to be your Fool now, Madam; you shan't impose upon me a second Time. I'll assure you, Madam, I know better Things. Besides he was wounded; and bled so fast that he wanted Assistance himself: And 'tis very probable, that the Sight of the *Babylonian* Couriers, who were dispatch'd from King *Moabdar*, might discompose him very much. He made all the Haste he could towards the Village, not being able to conceive what should be the real Cause of the young Lady's being secur'd by those *Babylonish* Officers, and as much at a Loss, at the same Time, what to think of such a Termagant and a Coquet.

CHAP. IX.

The CAPTIVE.

N o sooner was *Zadig* arriv'd at the *Egyptian* Village before-mention'd, but he found himself surrounded by a Croud. The People one and all cried out! See! See! there's the Man that ran away with the beauteous Lady *Missouf*, and murder'd *Cletofis*. Gentlemen, said he, God forbid that I should ever entertain a Thought of running away with the Lady you speak of: She is too much of a Coquet: And as to *Cletofis*, I did not murder him, but kill'd him in my own Defence. He endeavour'd all he could to take my Life away, because I entreated him to take some Pity and Compassion on the beauteous *Missouf*, whom he beat most unmercifully. I am a Stranger, who am fled hither for Shelter, and 'tis highly improbable, that upon my first Entrance into a Country, where I came for Safety and Protection, I should be guilty of two such enormous Crimes, as that of running away with another Man's Partner, and that of clandestinely murdering him on her Account.

The *Egyptians* at that Time were just and humane. The Populace, tis true, hurried *Zadig* to the Town-Goal; but they took care in the first Place to stop the Bleeding of his Wounds, and afterwards examin'd the suppos'd Delinquents apart, in order to discover, if possible, the real Truth. They acquitted *Zadig* of the Charge of wilful and premeditated Murder; but as he had taken a Subject's Life away, tho' in his own Defence, he was sentenc'd to be a Slave, as the Law directed. His two Beasts were sold in open Market, for the Service of the Hamlet; What Money he had was distributed amongst the Inhabitants; and he and his Attendant were expos'd in the Market-place to public Sale. An *Arabian* Merchant, *Setoc* by Name, purcha'd them both; but as the Valet, or Attendant, was a robust Man, and better cut out for hard Labour than the Master, he fetch'd the most Money. There was no Comparison to be made between them. *Zadig* therefore was a Slave subordinate to his Valet; they secur'd them both, however, by a Chain upon their Legs; and so link'd they accompanied their Master home. *Zadig*, as they were on the Road, comforted his Fellow-Slave, and exhorted him to bear his Misfortunes with Patience: But, according to Custom, he made several Reflections on the Vicissitudes of human Life. I am now sensible, said he, that my impropitious Fortune has some malignant Influence over thine; every Occurrence of my Life hitherto has prov'd strangely odd and unaccountable. In the first Place, I was sentenc'd to die at *Babylon*, for writing a short Panegyrick on the King, my Master. In the next, I narrowly escap'd being strangled, for the Queen his Royal Consort's speaking a little too much in my

Favour; and here I am a joint-Slave with thy self; because a turbulent Fellow of a Gallant would beat his Lady. However, Comrade, let us march on boldly; let not our Courage be cast down; all this may possibly have a happier Issue than we expect. 'Tis absolutely necessary that these *Arabian* Merchants should have Slaves, and why should not you and I, as we are but Men, be Slaves as Thousands of others are? This Master of ours may not prove inexorable. He must treat his Slaves with some Thought and Consideration, if he expects them to do his Work. This was his Discourse to his Comrade; but his Mind was more attentive to the Misfortunes of the Queen of *Babylon*.

Two Days afterwards *Setoc* set out with his two Slaves and his Camels, for *Arabia Deserta*. His Tribe liv'd near the Desert of *Horeb*. The Way was long and tedious. *Setoc*, during the Journey, paid a much greater Regard to *Zadig*'s Valet, than to himself; because the former was the most able to load the Camels; and therefore what little Distinctions were made, they were in his Favour. It so happen'd that one of the Camels died upon the Road: The Load which the Beast carried was immediately divided, and thrown upon the Shoulders of the two Slaves; *Zadig* had his Share. *Setoc*, couldn't forbear laughing to see his two Slaves crouching under their Burthen. *Zadig* took the Liberty to explain the Reason thereof; and convinc'd him of the Laws of the Equilibrium. The Merchant was a little startled at his philosophical Discourse, and look'd upon him with a more favourable Eye than at first. *Zadig*, perceiving he had rais'd his Curiosity, redoubled it, by instructing him in several material Points, which were in some Measure, advantageous to him in his Way of Business: Such as, the specific Weight of Metals, and other Commodities of various Kinds, of an equal Bulk; the Properties of several useful Animals, and the best Ways and Means to make Such as were wild, tame by Degrees, and fit for Service: In short, *Zadig* was look'd upon by his Master, as a perfect Oracle. *Setoc* now thought the Master the much better Man of the two. He us'd him courteously, and had no Room to repent of his Indulgence towards him.

Being got to their Journey's End, the first Step that *Setoc* took was to claim a Debt of five hundred Ounces of Silver of a *Jew*, who had borrow'd it in the Presence of two Witnesses; but both of them were dead; and as the *Jew* was conscious he couldn't be cast for Want of Evidence, appropriated the Merchant's Money to his own Use, and thank'd God that it lay in his Power for once to bite an *Arabian* with Impunity. *Setoc* discover'd to *Zadig* the unhappy Situation of his Case, as he was now become his Confident. Where was it, pray, said *Zadig*, that you lent this large Sum to that ungrateful Infidel? Upon a large Stone, said the Merchant, at the Foot of Mount *Horeb*. What sort of a Man is your Debtor, said *Zadig*? Oh! he is as errand a Rogue as ever breath'd, reply'd *Setoc*. That I take for granted; but, says *Zadig*, is he a lively, active Man, or is he a dull heavy-headed Fellow? He is one of the worst of Pay-masters in the World, but the merriest, most sprightly Fellow I ever met with. Very well! said *Zadig*, let me be one of your Council when your Cause comes to be heard. In short, he summon'd the *Jew* to attend the Court; where, when the Judge was sat, *Zadig* open'd the Cause: Thou impartial Judge of this Court of Equity, I am come here, in behalf of my Master, to demand of the Defendant five hundred Ounces of Silver, which he refuses to pay, and would fain traverse the Debt. Have you, Friend, your Witnesses ready to prove the Loan, said the Judge? No, they are dead; but there is a large Stone still subsisting, on which the Money was deposited; and if your Excellence, will be pleas'd to order the Stone to be brought in Court, I don't doubt but the Evidence it will give, will be Proof sufficient of the Fact. I hope your Excellence will order, that the *Jew* and myself shall be oblig'd to attend the Court, till the Stone comes, and I'll dispatch a special Messenger to fetch it, at my Master's Expence. Your Request is very reasonable, said the Judge. Do as you propose; and so call'd another Cause.

When the Court was ready to break up, Well! said the Judge to *Zadig*, is your Stone come yet? The *Jew*, with a Sneer, replied, your Excellence may wait here till this Time To-morrow, before the Stone will appear in Court; for 'tis above six Mile off, and it will require fifteen Men to remove it from its Place. 'Tis well! replied *Zadig*. I told your Excellence that the Stone would be a very material Evidence. Since the Defendant can point out the Place where the Stone lies, he tacitly confesses, that it was upon that Stone the Money was deposited. The *Jew* thus unexpectedly confuted, was soon oblig'd to acknowledge the Debt. The Judge order'd that the *Jew* should be tied fast to the Stone, without Victuals or Drink, till he should advance the five hundred Ounces of Silver, which were soon paid accordingly, and the *Jew* releas'd. The Slave *Zadig*, and this remarkable Stone-Witness, were in great Repute all over *Arabia*.

CHAP. X.

The FUNERAL PILE.

S etoc, transported with his good Success, of a Slave made *Zadig* his Favourite Companion and Confident; he found him as necessary in the Conduct of his Affairs, as the King of *Babylon* had before done in the Administration of his Government; and lucky it was for *Zadig* that *Setoc* had no Wife.

He discover'd, that his Master was in his Temper benevolent, strictly honest, and a Man of good natural Parts. *Zadig* was very much concern'd, that One of so much Sense should pay divine Adoration to a whole Host of created, tho' Celestial Beings, that is to say, the Sun, Moon, and Stars, according to the antient Custom of the *Arabians*. He talk'd, at first, to his Master, with great Precaution on so important a Topick. But at last told him, in direct Terms, that they were created Bodies, as others, tho' of less Lustre, and that there was no more Adoration due to them, than to a Stock or a Stone. But, said *Setoc*, they are eternal Beings to whom we are indebted for all the Blessings we enjoy; they animate Nature; they regulate the Seasons; they are, in a Word, at such an infinite Distance from us, that it would be downright impious not to adore them. You are more indebted, said *Zadig*, to the Waters of the Red Sea, which transport so many valuable Commodities into the *Indies*. Why, pray, may not they be deem'd as antient as the Stars? And if you are so fond of paying your Adoration on Account of their vast Distance; why don't you adore the Land of the *Gangarides*, which lies in the utmost Extremities of the Earth. No, said *Setoc*, there is something so surprisingly more brilliant in the Stars than what you speak of; that a Man must adore them whether he will or not.

At the Close of the Evening, *Zadig* planted a long Range of Candles in the Front of his Tent, where *Setoc* and he were to sup that Night: And as soon as he perceiv'd his Patron to be at the Door, he fell prostrate on his Knees before the Wax-Lights. O ye everlasting, ever-shining Luminaries, be always propitious to your Votary, said *Zadig*. Having repeated these Words so loud as *Setoc* might hear them, he sat down to Table, without taking the least Notice of *Setoc*. What! said *Setoc*, somewhat startled at his Conduct, art thou at thy Prayers before Supper? I act just as inconsistently, Sir, as you do; I worship these Candles; without reflecting on their Makers, or yourself, who are my most beneficent Patron.

Setoc took the Hint, and was conscious of the Reproof that was conceal'd so genteely under a Vail. The superior Wisdom of his Slave enlightned his Mind;

and from that Hour he was less lavish than ever he had been, of his Incense to those created Beings, and for the future, paid his Adoration to the eternal God who made them.

At that Time there was a most hideous Custom in high Repute all over *Arabia*, which came originally from *Scythia*; but having met with the Sanction of the bigotted Brachmans, threatn'd to spread its Infection all over the *East*. When a married Man happen'd to die, if his dearly beloved Widow ever expected to be esteem'd a Saint, she must throw herself headlong upon her Husband's Funeral-Pile. This was look'd upon as a solemn Festival, and was call'd the Widow's Sacrifice. That Tribe which could boast of the greatest Number of burnt-Widows, was look'd upon as the most meritorious. An *Arabian*, who was of the Tribe of *Setoc*, happen'd just at that Juncture, to be dead, and his Widow (*Almona* by Name) who was a noted Devotee, publish'd the Day, nay, the Hour, that she propos'd to throw herself (according to Custom) on her deceased Husband's Funeral Pile, and be attended by a Concert of Drums and Trumpets. *Zadig* remonstrated to *Setoc*, what a shocking Custom this was, and how directly repugnant to human Nature; by permitting young Widows, almost every Day, to become wilful Self- Murderers; when they might be of Service to their Country, either by the Addition of new Subjects, or by the Education of such as demanded their Maternal Indulgence. And, by arguing seriously with *Setoc* for some Time, he forc'd from him at last, an ingenuous Confession, that the barbarous Custom then subsisting, ought, if possible, to be abolish'd. 'Tis now, replied *Setoc*, above a thousand Years since the Widows of *Arabia* have been indulg'd with this Privilege of dying with their Husbands; and how shall any one dare to abrogate a Law that has been establish'd Time out of Mind? Is there any Thing more inviolable than even an antient Error? But, replied *Zadig*, Reason is of more antient Date than the Custom you plead for. Do you communicate these Sentiments to the Sovereigns of your Tribes, and in the mean while I'll go, and sound the Widow's Inclinations.

Accordingly he paid her a Visit, and having insinuated himself into her Favour, by a few Compliments on her Beauty, after urging what a pity it was, that a young Widow, Mistress of so many Charms, should make away with herself for no other reason but to mingle her Ashes with a Husband that was dead; he, notwithstanding, applauded her for her heroic Constancy and Courage. I perceive, Madam, said he, you was excessively fond of your deceased Spouse. Not I truly, reply'd the young *Arabian* Devotee. He was a Brute, infected with a groundless Jealousy of my Virtue; and, in short, a perfect Tyrant. But, notwithstanding all this, I am determin'd to comply with our Custom. Surely then, Madam, there's a Sort of secret Pleasure in being burnt alive. Alas! with a Sigh, cried *Almona*, 'tis a Shock indeed to Nature;

but must be complied with for all that. I am a profess'd Devotee, and should I shew the least Reluctance, my Reputation would be lost for ever; all the World would laugh at me, should I not burn myself on this Occasion: *Zadig* having forc'd her ingenuously to confess, that she parted with her Life more out of Regard to what the World would say of her, and out of Pride and Ostentation, than any real Love for the deceas'd, he talk'd to her for some considerable Time so rationally, and us'd so many prevailing Arguments with her to justify her due Regard for the Life which she was going to throw away, that she began to wave the Thought, and entertain a secret Affection for her friendly Monitor. Pray, Madam, tell me, said *Zadig*, how would you dispose of yourself, upon the Supposition, that you could shake off this vain and barbarous Notion? Why, said Dame, with an amorous Glance, I think verily I should accept of yourself for a second Bed-fellow.

The Memory of *Astarte* had made too strong an Impression on his Mind, to close with this warm Declaration: He took his leave, however, that Moment, and waited on the Chiefs. He communicated to them the Substance of their private Conversation, and prevailed with them to make it a Law for the future, that no Widow should be allow'd to fall a Victim to a deceased Husband, till after she had admitted some young Man to converse with her in private for a whole Hour together. The Law was pass'd accordingly, and not one Widow in all *Arabia*, from that Day to this, ever observ'd the Custom. 'Twas to *Zadig* alone that the *Arabian* Dames were indebted for the Abolition, in one Hour, of a Custom so very inhuman, that had been practis'd for such a Number of Ages. *Zadig*, therefore, with the strictest Justice, was look'd upon by all the Fair Sex in *Arabia*, as their most bountiful Benefactor.

CHAP. XI.

The Evening's Entertainment.

S etoc, who would never stir out without his Bosom-Friend (in whom alone, as he thought, all Wisdom center'd) resolv'd to take him with him to *Balzora* Fair, whither the richest Merchants round the whole habitable Globe, us'd annually to resort. *Zadig* was delighted to see such a Concourse of substantial Tradesmen from all Countries, assembled together in one Place. It appear'd to him, as if the whole Universe was but one large Family, and all happily met together at *Balzora*. On the second Day of the Fair, he sat down to Table with an *Egyptian*, an *Indian*, that liv'd on the Banks of the River *Ganges*, an Inhabitant of *Cathay*, a *Grecian*, a *Celt*, and several other Foreigners, who by their frequent Voyages towards the *Arabian* Gulf, were so far conversant with the *Arabic* Language, as to be able to discourse freely, and be mutually understood. The *Egyptian* began to fly into a Passion; what a scandalous Place is this *Balzora*, said he, where they refuse to lend me a thousand Ounces of Gold, upon the best Security that can possibly be offer'd. Pray, said *Setoc*, what may the Commodity be that you would deposit as a Pledge for the Sum you mention. Why, the Corpse of my deceased Aunt, said he, who was one of the finest Women in all *Egypt*. She was my constant Companion; but unhappily died upon the Road. I have taken so much Care, that no Mummy whatever can equal it: And was I in my own Country, I could be furnish'd with what Sum soever I pleas'd, were I dispos'd to mortgage it. 'Tis a strange Thing that Nobody here will advance so small a Sum upon so valuable a Commodity. No sooner had he express'd his Resentment, but he was going to cut up a fine boil'd Pullet, in order to make a Meal on't, when an *Indian* laid hold of his Hand, and with deep Concern, cried out, For God's Sake what are you about? Why, said the *Egyptian*, I design to make a Wing of this Fowl one Part of my Supper. Pray, good Sir, consider what you are doing, said the *Indian*. 'Tis very possible, that the Soul of the deceas'd Lady may have taken its Residence in that Fowl. And you wouldn't surely run the Risque of eating up your Aunt? To boil a Fowl is, doubtless, a most shameful Outrage done to Nature. Pshaw! What a Pother you make about the boiling of a Fowl, and flying in the Face of Nature, replied the *Egyptian* in a Pet; tho' we *Egyptians* pay divine Adoration to the Ox; yet we can make a hearty Meal of a Piece of roast Beef for all that. Is it possible, Sir, that your Country-men should act so absurdly, as to pay an Ox the Tribute of divine Worship, said the *Indian*? Absurd as you think it, said the other, the Ox has been the principal Object of Adoration all over *Egypt*, for these hundred and thirty five thousand

Years, and the most abandon'd *Egyptian* has never been as yet so impious as to gain-say it. Ay, Sir, an hundred thirty five thousand Years, say you, surely you must be out a little in your Calculation. 'Tis but about fourscore thousand Years, since *India* was first inhabited. Sure I am, we are a more antient People than you are, and our *Brama* prohibited the eating of Beef long before your Nation ever erected an Altar in Honour of the Ox, or ever put one upon a Spit. What a Racket you make about your *Brama*! Is he able to stand the least in Competition with our *Apis*, said the *Egyptian*? Let us hear, pray, what mighty Feats have been done by your boasted *Brama*? Why, replied the *Bramin*, he first taught his Votaries to write and read; and 'tis to him alone, all the World is indebted for the Invention of the noble Game of Chess. You are quite out, Sir, in your Notion, said a *Chaldean*, who sat within Hearing: All these invaluable Blessings were deriv'd from the Fish *Oannés*; and 'tis that alone to which the Tribute of divine Adoration is justly due. All the World will tell you, that 'twas a divine Being whose Tail was pure Gold, whose Head resembled that of a Man, tho' indeed the Features were much more beautiful; and that he condescended to visit the Earth three Hours every Day, for the Instruction of Mankind. He had a numerous Issue, as is very well known, and all of them were powerful Monarchs. I have a Picture of it at Home, to which, as in Duty I ought, I Say my Prayers at Night before I go to Bed, and every Morning that I rise. There is no Harm, Sir, as I can conceive, in partaking of a Piece of roast Beef; but, doubtless, 'tis a mortal Sin, a Crime of the blackest Dye, to touch a Piece of Fish. Besides, you cannot justly boast of so illustrious an Origin, and you are both of you mere Moderns, in Comparison to us *Chaldeans*, You *Egyptians* lay claim to no more than 135,000 Years, and you *Indians*, but of 80,000. Whereas we have Almanacks that are dated 4000 Centuries backwards. Take my Word for it; I speak nothing but Truth; renounce your Errors, and I'll make each of you a Present of a fine Portrait of our *Oannés*.

A Native of *Cambalu*, entring into the Debate, said, I have a very great Veneration, not only for the *Egyptians*, *Chaldeans*, *Greeks*, and *Celtæ*; but for *Brama*, *Apis*, and the *Oannés*, but in my humble Opinion, the *Li*, * The Chinese Term, Li, *signifies, properly speaking, natural Light, or Reason; and* Tien, *the Heavens, or the supreme Being.* or as 'tis by some call'd, the *Tien*, is an Object more deserving of divine Adoration than any Ox, or Fish, how much soever you may boast of their respective Perfections. All I shall say, in regard to my native Country, 'tis of much greater Extent, than all *Egypt*, *Chaldea*, and the *Indies* put together. I shall lay no Stress on the Antiquity of my Country; for I imagine 'tis of much greater Importance to be the happiest People, than the most antient under the Sun. However, since you were talking of the Almanacks, I must beg the Liberty to tell you, that ours are look'd upon to be the best all over *Asia*; and that we had several very correct ones before the Art of

Arithmetick was ever heard of in *Chaldea*.

You are all of you a Parcel of illiterate, ignorant Bigots, cry'd a *Grecian*: 'Tis plain, you know nothing of the Chaos, and that the World, as it now stands, is owing wholly to *Matter* and *Form*. The *Greek* ran on for a considerable Time; but was at last interrupted by a *Celt*, who having drank deep, during the whole Time of this Debate, thought himself ten Times wiser than any of his Antagonists; and wrapping out a great Oath, insisted, that all their Gods were nothing, if set in Competition with the *Teutath* or the Misletoe on the Oak. As for my part, said he, I carry some of it always in my Pocket: As to my Ancestors, they were *Scythians*, and the only Men worth talking of in the whole World: 'Tis true, indeed, they would now and then make a Meal of their Country-men, but that ought not to be urg'd as any Objection to his Country; and, in short, if any one of you, or all of you, shall dare to say any thing disrespectful of *Teutath*, I'll defend its Cause to the last Drop of my Blood. The Quarrel grew warmer and warmer, and *Setoc* expected that the Table would be overset, and that Blood-shed would ensue. *Zadig*, who hadn't once open'd his Lips during the whole Controversy, at last rose up, and address'd himself to the *Celt*, in the first Place, as being the most noisy and outrageous. Sir, said he, Your Notions in this Affair are very just: Good Sir, oblige me with a Bit of your Misletoe. Then turning about, he expatiated on the Eloquence of the *Grecian*, and in a Word, soften'd in the most artful Manner all the contending Parties. He said but little indeed to the *Cathayian*; because he was more cool, and sedate than any of the others. To conclude, he address'd them all in general Terms, to this or the like Effect: My dear Friends, You have been contesting all this while about an important Topick, in which 'tis evident, you are all unanimously agreed. Agreed, quotha! they all cried, in an angry Tone, How so, pray? Why said he to the hot, testy *Celt*, is it not true, that you do not in effect adore this Misletoe, but that Being who created that Misletoe and the Oak, to which it is so closely united? Doubtless, Sir, reply'd the *Celt*. And you, Sir, said he, to the *Egyptian*, You revere, thro' your venerable *Apis*, the great Author of every Ox's Being. We do so, said the *Egyptian*. The mighty *Oannés*, tho' the Sovereign of the Sea, continued he, must give Precedence to that Power, who made both the Sea, and every Fish that dwells therein. We allow it, said the *Chaldean*. The *Indian*, adds he, and the *Cathayan*, acknowledge one supreme Being, or first Cause, as well as you. As to what that profound worthy Gentleman the *Grecian* has advanc'd, is, I must own, a little above my weak Comprehension, but I am fully persuaded, that he will allow there is a supreme Being on whom his favourite Matter and Form are entirely dependent. The *Grecian*, who was look'd upon as a Sage amongst them, said, with Abundance of Gravity, that *Zadig*, had made a very just Construction of his Meaning. Now, Gentlemen, I appeal to you all, said *Zadig*, whether you are not unanimous to a Man, in the Debate upon the Carpet, and whether there are any just Grounds for the least Divisions or Animosities amongst you. The whole Company, cool at once, caress'd him; and *Setoc*, after he had sold off all his Goods and Merchandize at a round Price, took his Friend *Zadig* Home with him to the Land of *Horeb*. *Zadig*, upon his first Arrival was inform'd, that a Prosecution had been carried on against him during his Absence, and that the Sentence pronounc'd against him was, that he should be burnt alive before a slow Fire.

CHAP. XII.

The RENDEZVOUS.

Whilst *Zadig* attended his Friend *Setoc* to *Balzora*, the Priests of the Stars were determin'd to punish him. As all the costly Jewels, and other valuable Decorations, in which every young Widow that sacrificed her self on her Husband's Funeral-pile, were their customary Fees, 'tis no great Wonder, indeed, that they were inclin'd to burn poor *Zadig*, for playing them such a scurvy Trick. *Zadig* therefore, was accus'd of holding heretical and damnable Tenets, in regard to the Celestial Host: They depos'd, and swore point-blank, that he had been heard to aver, that the Stars never sat in the Sea. This horrid blasphemous Declaration thunder-struck all the Judges, and they were ready to rend their Mantles at the Sound of such an impious Assertion; and they would have made *Zadig*, had he been a Man of Substance, paid very severely for his heretical Notions. But in the Height of their Pity and Compassion for even such an Infidel, they would lay no Fine upon him; but content themselves with seeing him roasted alive before a slow Fire. *Setoc*, tho' without Hopes of Success, us'd all the Interest he had to save his bosom Friend from so shocking a Death; but they turn'd a deaf Ear to all his Remonstrances, and oblig'd him to hold his Tongue. The young Widow *Almona*, who by this Time was not only reconcil'd to living a little longer, but had some Taste for the Pleasures of Life, and knew that she was entirely indebted to *Zadig* for it, resolv'd, if possible, to free her Benefactor from being burnt, as he had before convinc'd her of the Folly of it in her Case. She ponder'd upon this weighty Affair very seriously; but said nothing to any one whomsoever. *Zadig* was to be executed the next Day; and she had only a few Hours left to carry her Project into Execution. Now the Reader shall hear with how much Benevolence and Discretion this amiable Widow behav'd on this emergent Occasion.

In the first Place, she made use of the most costly Perfumes; and drest herself to the utmost Advantage to render her Charms as conspicuous as possible; And thus gaily attir'd, demanded a private Audience of the High Priest of the Stars. Upon her first Admittance into his august and venerable Presence, she address'd herself in the following Terms. O thou first-born and well-beloved Son of the Great Bear, Brother of the Bull, and first Cousin to the Dog, (these you must know were the Pontiff's high Titles) I come to confess myself before you: My Conscience is my Accuser, and I am terribly afraid I have been guilty of a mortal Sin, by declining the stated Custom of burning my self on my Husband's Funeral-pile? What could tempt me, in short, to a

Prolongation of my Life, I can't imagine, I, who am grown a perfect Skeleton, all wrinkled and deform'd. She paus'd, and pulling off, with a negligent but artful Air, her long silk Gloves; She display'd a soft, plump, naked Arm, and white as Snow: You see, Sir, said she, that all my Charms are blasted. Blasted, Madam, said the luscious Pontiff; No! Your Charms are still resistless: His Eyes, and his Mouth, with which he kiss'd her Hand, confirm'd their Power: Such an Arm, Madam, by the Great *Orasmades*, I never saw before. Alas! said the Widow, with a modest Blush; my Arm Sir, 'tis probable, may have the Advantage of any hidden Part; but see, good Father, what a Neck is here; as yellow as Saffron, an Object not worth regarding. Then she display'd such a snowy, panting Bosom, that Nature could not mend it. A Rose-Bud on an Ivory Apple, would, if set in Competition with her spotless Whiteness, make no better Appearance than common Madder upon a Shrub; and the whitest Wool, just out of the Laver, were she but by, would seem but of a light-brown Hue.

Her Neck, her large black, sparkling Eyes, that languishingly roll'd, and seem'd as 'twere, on Fire; her lovely Cheeks, glowing with White and Red, her Nose, that was not unlike the Tower of Mount *Lebanon*, her Lips, which were like two Borders of Coral, inclosing two Rows of the best Pearls in the *Arabian* Sea; such a Combination, I say, of Charms, made the old Pontiff judge she was scarce twenty Years of Age; and in a kind of Flutter, to make her a Declaration of his tender Regard for her. *Almona*, perceiving him enamour'd, begg'd his Interest in Favour of *Zadig*. Alas! my dear Charmer, my Interest alone, when you request the Favour, would be but a poor Compliment; I'll take care his Acquittance shall be signed by three more of my Brother Priests. Do you sign first, however, said *Almona*. With all my Soul, said the amorous Pontiff, provided——you'll be kind, my dearest. You do me too much Honour, said *Almona*; but should you give your self the Trouble to pay me a Visit after Sunset, and as soon as the Star *Sheat* twinkles on the Horizon, you shall find me, most venerable Father, repos'd upon a rosy-colour'd silver Sopha, where you shall use your Pleasure with your humble Servant. With that she made him a low Courtesy; took up *Zadig*'s general Release as soon as duely sign'd, and left the old Doatard all over Love, tho' somewhat diffident of his own Abilities. The Residue of the Day he spent in his Bagnio; he drank large enlivening Draughts of a Water distill'd from the Cinnamon of *Ceilan*, and the costly Spices of *Tidor* and *Ternate*, and waited with the utmost Impatience for the up-rising of the brilliant *Sheat*.

In the mean time *Almona* went to the second Pontiff. He assur'd her that the Sun, Moon, and all the starry Host of Heav'n, were but languid Fires to her bright Eyes. He put the Question to her, in short, at once, and agreed to sign upon her Compliance. She suffer'd herself to be over-persuaded, and made an

Assignation to meet him at a certain Place, as soon as the Star *Algenib* should make its Appearance. From him she repair'd to the third and fourth Pontiff, taking care, wherever she went, to see *Zadig*'s Acquittance duely sign'd, and made fresh Appointments at the Rising of Star after Star.

When she had carried her Point thus far, she sent a proper Message to the Judges of the Court, who had condemn'd *Zadig*, requesting that they would come to her House, that she might advise with them upon an Affair of the last Importance. They waited on her accordingly; she produc'd *Zadig*'s Discharge duly sign'd by four several Hands, and told them the Definitive Treaty between all the contracting Parties. Each of the pontifical Gallants observ'd their Summons to a Moment. Each was startled at the Sight of his Rival; but perfectly thunderstruck to see the Judges, before whom the Widow had laid open her Case. *Zadig* procur'd an absolute Pardon, and *Setoc* was so charm'd with the artful Address of *Almona*, that he married her the next Day. *Zadig* went afterwards to throw himself at the Feet of his fair Benefactress. *Setoc* and he took their Leave of each other with Tears in their Eyes, and vowing that an eternal mutual Friendship should be preserv'd between them; and, in short, should Fortune at any Time afterwards prove more propitious than could well be expected to either Party; the other should partake of an equal Share of his Success.

Zadig steer'd his Course towards *Syria*; forever pondering on the hard Fate of the justly-admir'd *Astarte*, and reflecting on his own Stars that so obstinately darted down their malignant Rays, and continu'd daily to torment him. What, said he! to pay four hundred Ounces of Gold for only seeing a Bitch pass by me; to be condemn'd to be beheaded for four witless Verses in Praise of the King; to be strangled to Death, because a Queen was pleas'd to look upon me; to be made a Prisoner, and sold as a Slave for saving a young Lady from being sorely abus'd by a Brute rather than a Man; and to be upon the Brink of being roasted alive, for no other Offence than saving for the future all the Widows in *Arabia* from becoming idle Burnt-Offerings, and mingling their Ashes with those of their deceased worthless Husbands.

CHAP. XIII.

The FREE-BOOTER.

*Z*adig, arriving at the Frontiers which separate *Arabia Petræa* from *Syria*, and passing by a very strong Castle, several arm'd *Arabians* rush'd out upon him, and surrounding him, cried out: Whatever you have belonging to you is our Property, but as for your Person, that is entirely at our Sovereign's Disposal. *Zadig*, instead of making any Reply, drew his Sword, and as his Attendant was a very couragious Fellow, he drew likewise. Those who laid hold on them, first fell a Sacrifice to their Fury: Their Numbers redoubled: Yet still, Both dauntless, determin'd to conquer or to die. When two Men defend themselves against a whole Gang, the Contest, doubtless, cannot last long. The Master of the Castle, one *Arbogad* by Name, having been an Eye-Witness from his Window, of the Intrepidity and surprising Exploits of *Zadig*, took a Fancy to him. He ran down therefore in Haste, and giving Orders himself to his Vassals to desist, deliver'd the two Travellers out of their Hands. Whatever Goods or Chattels, said he, come upon my Territories, are my Effects; and whatever I find likewise that is valuable upon the Premises of others, is my free Booty; but, as you appear, Sir, to me to be a Gentleman of uncommon Courage, you shall prove an Exception to my general Rule. Upon this, he invited *Zadig* into his magnificent Mansion, giving his inferior Officers strict Orders to use him with all due Respect; and at Night *Arbogad* was desirous of supping with *Zadig*. The Lord of the Mansion was one of those *Arabians*, that are call'd *Free-booters*; but a Man who now and then did good Actions amongst a Thousand bad ones. He plunder'd without Mercy; but was liberal in his Benefactions. When in Action, intrepid; but in Traffick, easy enough; a perfect *Epicure* in his Eating and Drinking, an absolute *Debauchee*, but very frank and open. *Zadig* pleas'd him extremely; his Conversation being very lively, prolong'd their Repast: At last, *Arbogad* said to him; I would advise you, Sir, to enlist yourself in my Troop; you cannot possibly do a better Thing: My Profession is none of the worst; and in Time, you may become perhaps as great a Man as myself. May I presume, Sir, to ask you one Question; how long may you have follow'd this honourable Calling? From my Youth upwards, replied his Host, I was only a *Valet* at first to an *Arabian*, who indeed was courteous enough; but Servitude was a State of Life I could not brook. It made me stark-mad to see, in a wide World, which ought to be divided fairly between Mankind, that Fate had reserv'd for me so scanty a Portion. I communicated my Grievance to an old Sage *Arabian*. Son, said he, never despair; once upon a Time, there was a Grain of

47

Sand, that bemoan'd itself, as being nothing more than a worthless *Atom* of the Deserts. At the Expiration, however, of a few Years, it became that inestimable Diamond, which at this very Hour, is the richest, and most admir'd Ornament of the *Indian* Crown. The old Man's Discourse fir'd me with some Ambition; I was conscious to myself that I was at that Time the *Atom* he mention'd, but was determin'd, if possible, to become the *Diamond*. At my first setting out, I stole two Horses; then I got into a Gang; where we play'd at small Game, and stopp'd the small Caravans; thus I gradually lessen'd the wide Disproportion, which there was at first between me and the rest of Mankind: I enjoy'd not only my full Share of the good Things of this Life, but enjoy'd them with Usury. I was look'd upon as a Man of Consequence, and I procur'd this Castle by my military Atchievements. The *Satrap* of *Syria* had Thoughts of dispossessing me; but I was then too rich to be any Ways afraid of him; I gave the *Satrap* a certain Sum of Money, upon Condition that I kept quiet Possession of my Castle. And, moreover, I aggrandiz'd my Domains; for he constituted me, at the same Time, Treasurer of the Imports that *Arabia Petræa* paid to the King of Kings. I executed my Trust, in every Respect, as I ought, in the Capacity of a Collector; but I never did, nor never intended to balance my Accounts.

The grand *Desterham* of *Babylon* sent hither, in the Name of the King *Moabdar*, a petty *Satrap*, with a Commission to strangle me. He and his Attendants arriv'd here with his Royal Warrant. I was appriz'd of the whole Affair, and, accordingly, order'd his whole Retinue, consisting of four inferior Officers, to be strangled before his Face, after the same Manner as was intended for my Execution. After this, I ask'd him what he thought the Commission with which he was entrusted, might reasonably be valued at; he answer'd, that he presum'd his Premium (had he succeeded) might have amounted to about three Hundred Pieces of Gold. I made him sensible, that it would be for his Interest to be a commission'd Officer under me; I made him accordingly Deputy *Free-booter*. He is at this very Day not only the best Officer, but the richest I have in all my Court. If my Word may be credited, I'll raise your Fortune as I have done his. Never was Trade brisker in our Way; for *Moabdar*, is knock'd on the Head, and all *Babylon* in the utmost Confusion. *Moabdar* kill'd, said you! cry'd *Zadig*, and pray, Sir, what is become of his Royal Consort, *Astarte*? I know nothing at all of that Affair, replied *Arbogad*, all that I have to say, is, that *Moabdar* became a perfect Madman, and had his Brains beat out; that all the People in *Babylon* are cutting one another's Throats, and that the whole Empire is laid waste; that there is still an Opportunity for making several bold Pushes; and let me tell you, Sir, I have done my Part, and made the most on't. But the Queen, Sir, said *Zadig*; pray favour me so far, as to inform me, if you know any Thing of the Queen. I have heard great Talk, said he, of a certain Prince of *Hyrcania*; 'tis very possible, she may have listed herself amongst his Concubines, if she had the good Fortune to escape the Resentment of those popular Tumults; but my Head, Sir, is better turn'd for the Highway than for News; I have taken several Ladies Prisoners in the Course of my Excursions; I keep none of them for my Part; and as to such as are handsomer than ordinary, I make the best Market I can of them, without enquiring who they are. Their Quality or Titles will fetch no Price at all; a Queen, if she be homely, is worth nothing. 'Tis probable, Sir, I have dispos'd of the Lady myself; and 'tis possible, likewise, she may be dead; 'tis no Concern of mine; and to my thinking, it should be an Affair of no Manner of Importance to you. After this Declaration, he drank so hard, and confounded his Ideas in such a Manner, that *Zadig* was not one whit the wiser. Upon which he was struck dumb, confounded, and stood as motionless as a Statue. *Arbogad*, in the mean while, swill'd down whole Bumpers, told a Hundred merry Tales, and swore a thousand Times over, that he was the happiest Creature upon God's Earth; persuading *Zadig* to be as merry, and thoughtless as himself. At last, being gradually overcome by the Fumes of his Liquor, he fell fast asleep. *Zadig* spent the Remainder of the Night in deep Contemplation, and in all the Uneasiness of Mind imaginable. What, said he, the King first became crazy, and then was murder'd. I think I have just Grounds for Complaint. The whole Empire is in Confusion, and torn to Pieces, and this Free-booter is as happy as a King. O Fortune! O Fate! a Highwayman as happy as a Monarch! and the most amiable Creature that Nature ever fram'd has suffer'd perhaps, an ignominious Death, or perhaps, is in a State of Life a thousand Times worse than Death itself! O *Astarte! Astarte!* What art thou become?

As soon as it was Break of Day he went out, and ask'd every one he saw if they knew any Thing of her: But the whole Gang were too intent upon other Matters, to return him any Answer. By Virtue of their Night's Excursions, they had brought in some fresh Booty, and were busy in dividing the Spoil. All the Favour he could procure, in their Hurry and Tumult, was, to go away without the least Examination. He took the Advantage of their Remissness, and mov'd off the Premises, but more overwhelm'd with Grief and deep Reflection than ever.

Zadig, in his March, was very restless and uneasy. His Thoughts were forever rolling on the unfortunate *Astarte*, the King of *Babylon*, his Bosom-Friend *Cador*, the happy *Free-booter*, *Arbogad*, the fair *Coquet*, that was taken Prisoner on the Confines of *Egypt*, by the *Babylonish* Courier; in a Word, on the various Scenes of Misfortunes and Disappointments, which he had successively met with.

CHAP. XIV.

The FISHERMAN.

W hen *Zadig* had travelled some few Leagues from *Arbogad's* Castle, he found himself arriv'd at the Banks of a little River; incessantly deploring, as he went along, his unhappy Fate, and looking upon himself as the very Picture of ill Luck. He perceiv'd at a little Distance a Fisherman, reclin'd on a verdant Bank by the River-side, trembling, scarce able to hold his Net in his Hand, (which he seem'd but little to regard) and with uplift Eyes, imploring Heaven's Assistance. I am, doubtless, said the poor Fisherman, the most unhappy Wretch that ever liv'd! No Merchant in all *Babylon*, it is very well known, was ever so noted for selling Cream-Cheeses as myself; and yet I am ruin'd to all Intents and Purposes. No Man of my Profession ever had a handsomer, more compleat Housewife, than my Dame was; but I have been treacherously depriv'd of her. I had still left a poor, pitiful Cottage, but that I saw plunder'd and destroy'd. I am cubb'd up here in a Cell; I have nothing to depend upon but my Fishery, and not one single Fish have I caught. Thou unfortunate Net! I'll never throw thee into the Water more: Much sooner will I throw myself in. No sooner were the Words out of his Mouth, but he started up, and ran to the River-side, like one that was resolutely bent to plunge in, and get rid of a miserable Life at once. Is it possible, said *Zadig*? Is there then the Man in Being more wretched than myself? His Benevolence, and good Will to save the poor Man's Life, was as quick as the Reflection he had just made! He ran to his Assistance; he laid hold of him; and ask'd him, with an Air of Pity and Concern, the Cause of his rash Intention. 'Tis an old saying, that a Person is less unhappy when he sees himself not singular in Misfortune. But if we will credit *Zoroaster*, this is not from a Principle of Malignity, but the Effect of a fatal Necessity. He was attracted, as it were, to any Person in Distress, as being One in the same unhappy Circumstances. The Transport of a happy Man, would be a Kind of Insult; but two Persons in bad Circumstances, are like two weak Shrubs, which, by propping up each other, are fenc'd against a Storm. Why are you thus cast down, said *Zadig* to the Fisherman? Never sink Man, under the Weight of your Burden. I can't help it, said the poor Fisherman; I have not the least Prospect of Redress. I was once, Sir, the tip-top Man of the whole Village of *Derlbach*, near *Babylon*, where I liv'd, and with the Help of my Wife, made the best Cream-Cheeses that were ever eaten in the *Persian* Empire. Her Majesty, the Queen *Astarte*, and the famous Prime-Minister *Zadig* were very fond of them. I serv'd the Court with about six Hundred of them, I went the other Day in Hopes of being paid; but before I had well got into the Suburbs of *Babylon*, I was inform'd, that not only the Queen, but *Zadig* too had privately left the Court: Whereupon I ran directly to *Zadig*'s House, tho' I never sat Eye on the Man in all my Life. There I found the Court-Marshals of the grand *Desterham*, plundering, by Virtue of his Majesty's Mandate, all his Effects, in the most loyal Manner. From thence I made the best of my Way to the Queen's Kitchin; where, applying my self to the Steward of her Household, and his inferior Officers; one of them told me she was dead; another, that she was confin'd in Prison; a third, indeed, said that she had made her Escape by Flight; all in general, however, assur'd me for my Comfort, that my Cheeses would never be paid for. From thence I went, with my Wife in my Hand, to Lord *Orcan*'s; who was another of my Court-Customers; of whom we begg'd for Shelter and Protection: The Favour, I confess, was readily granted to my Wife; but as for my own Part, I was absolutely rejected. She was fairer, Sir, than the fairest Cheese I ever sold; from whence I date all my Misfortunes; and the red that adorn'd her blushing Cheeks was ten Times more lively than any *Tyrian* Scarlet. And between you and I, Sir, that was the main Cause of my Wife's Reception, and my Disgrace. Whereupon I wrote a doleful Letter to my Wife, in all the Agonies of one in the deepest Despair: 'Tis very well, said she, to the Messenger; I have some little Knowledge of the Man; I have heard say no one sells better Cream-Cheeses than he does; desire him, next Time he comes, to bring a small Parcel with him, and let him know, I'll take care he shall be punctually paid.

In the Height of my Misfortunes, I determin'd to seek Redress in a Court of Equity: I had but six Ounces of Gold left: Two whereof went for a Fee to my Counsellor; two to my Lawyer, who took my Cause in Hand, and the other two to the Judge's Clerk. Notwithstanding what I had done, my Cause was not so much as commenc'd; and I had already disburs'd more Money than all my Cheeses and my Wife with them were worth. I return'd therefore to my Native Habitation, with a full Resolution to sell it for the Ransom of my Wife.

My little Cot, with the Appurtenances, were worth about threescore Ounces of Gold: But as the Purchasers found I was necessitous, and drove to my last Shifts; the first whom I apply'd to, offer'd me thirty Ounces; the second, twenty; and the third, but ten: Just as I had come to Terms of Accommodation with one of them, the Prince of *Hyrcania* came to *Babylon*, and swept all before him. My little Cottage, with all its Furniture, was first plunder'd of all that was valuable, and at last reduc'd to Ashes.

Having thus lost my Money, my Wife, and my House, I withdrew to this Desart, where you see me. I have since endeavour'd to get my Bread by Fishing; but the Fish, as well as all Mankind, desert me. I scarce catch one in a Day; I am half starv'd; and had it not been for your unexpected Benevolence and Generosity, I had been at the Bottom of the River before this.

This long Detail of Particulars, however, was not deliver'd without several Interruptions; for, said *Zadig*, with Abundance of Warmth and Confusion, Have you never heard, Sir, of what is become of the Queen *Astarte*? No Sir, not I, said the disconsolate Fisherman; but this I know, to my Sorrow, that neither the Queen, nor *Zadig*, ever paid me the least Consideration in the World for my Cream Cheeses; that my dear Spouse is taken from me; and that I am drove to the very Brink of Despair. I am verily persuaded, said *Zadig*, that you will not lose all your Money. I have heard much talk of that same *Zadig*; they say he is very honest, and that if ever he returns to *Babylon*, as 'tis to be hop'd he will, he'll discharge his Debts with Interest, like a Man of Honour. But, as for your Wife, who appears to me, to be no better than a Wag- tail, never take the Trouble, if you'll take my Advice, to hunt after her any more. Be rul'd, and make the best of your Way to *Babylon*. I shall be there before you, as I shall ride, and you will be on Foot. Make your Applications to the illustrious *Cador*; tell him you met his Friend upon the Road; and stay there still I come. Observe my Orders, and 'tis very probable it may turn out to your Advantage.

O puissant *Orosmades*, continu'd he, you have made me, 'tis true, an Instrument of Comfort to this poor Man; but what Friend will you raise for me, to alleviate my Sorrows? Having utter'd this short Expostulation, he gave the distrest Fisherman one full Moiety of all the Money he brought with him out of *Arabia*. The Fisherman, thunder-struck, and transported with Joy at so unexpected a Benefaction, kiss'd the Feet of *Cador*'s Friend, and cried out, sure you are a Messenger of Heaven, sent down to be my Saviour!

In the mean Time, *Zadig* every now and then ask'd him Questions, and wept as he ask'd them. What! Sir, said the Fisherman, can you, who are so bountiful a Benefactor, be in Distress yourself? Alas! said he, Friend, I am a hundred Times more unhappy than thou art. But pray, Sir, said the good Man, how can it possibly be, that he, who is so lavish of his Favours, should be overwhelm'd with greater Misfortunes than the Man he so generously relieves? Your greatest Uneasiness, said he, arose from the Narrowness of your Circumstances; but mine proceeds from an internal, and much deeper Cause. Pray, Sir, said the Fisherman, has *Orcan* robb'd you of your Wife? This Interrogatory put *Zadig* in a Moment upon a Retrospection of all his past Adventures. He recollected the whole Series of his Misfortunes; commencing from that of the Eunuch and the Huntsman, to his Arrival at the Free-booter's Castle. Alas! said he, to the Fisherman, *Orcan*, 'tis true, deserves severely to be punish'd: But for the Generality, we find, such worthless Barbarians are the Favourites of Fortune. Be that, however, as it will, go as I bade you, to my Friend *Cador*, and wait there till I come. They took their Leave; the Fisherman blessing his propitious Stars, and *Zadig* cursing, every Step he went, the Hour he was born.

CHAP. XV.

The BASILISK.

A s *Zadig* was traversing a verdant Meadow, he perceiv'd several young Female *Syrians*, intent on searching for something very curious, that lay conceal'd, as they imagin'd, in the Grass. He took the Freedom to approach one of them, and ask her, in the most courteous Manner, if he might have the Honour to assist her in her Researches. Have a care, said she. What we are hunting after, Sir, is an Animal, that will not suffer itself to be touch'd by a Man. 'Tis somewhat surprizing, said *Zadig*. May I be so bold, pray, as to ask you what you are in Pursuit after, that shuns the Touch of any Thing but the Hands of the Fair Sex. 'Tis, Sir, said she, the *Basilisk*: A *Basilisk*, Madam, said he! And pray, if you will be so good as to inform me, with what View, are you searching after a Creature so very difficult to be met with? 'Tis, Sir, said she, for our Lord and Master *Ogul*, whose Castle, you see, situate on the River-side, at the Bottom of the Meadow. We are all his Vassals. *Ogul*, you must know, is in a very bad State of Health, and his first Physician has order'd him, as a Specific, to eat a *Basilisk*, boil'd in Rose water: And as that Animal is very hard to be catch'd, and will suffer nothing to approach it, but one of our Sex, our dying Sovereign *Ogul* has promis'd to honour her, that shall be so happy as to catch it for him, so far as to make her his Consort. The Case, being thus circumstantiated, Sir, I hope you will not interrupt me any longer, lest my Rivals here in the Field should happen to circumvent me.

Zadig withdrew, and left the *Syrian* Ladies in Quest of their imaginary Booty, in order to pursue his intended Journey. But as he came to the Banks of a Rivulet, at the remotest part of the Meadow, he perceiv'd another young Lady, reclin'd on the Grass, and entirely disengag'd. Her Stature seem'd majestic, but her Face was cover'd with a Vail; and her Eyes were fixt, as one at her Looking-glass, on the River. Every now and then a Sigh burst out, as if her Heart were breaking. In her Hand she held a little Wand or Rod, with which she was tracing out some Characters on the dry Sand, that lay between the flow'ry Bank she sat on, and the purling Current. *Zadig*'s Curiosity induc'd him, unperceiv'd, to observe her Operations at some Distance. But approaching nearer, and perceiving very distinctly the first Character to be an *Z*. the next an *A*. and the third a *D*. he started; but when he saw the additional Capitals of *I* and *G*. his Astonishment was too great for Words to express. He stood for some Time perfectly thunder-struck, and as motionless as a Statue; At last, in a soft, faultring Tone, he broke Silence: O generous Lady, said he, forgive a Stranger, one overwhelm'd with Sorrows like yourself, if he asks you, by what amazing Accident he finds the Name of *Zadig* delineated by so angelick a Hand. Thus unexpectedly interrupted, and at the Sound of those Words, she turn'd her Head; and with a trembling Hand, lifting up her Vail, she espy'd *Zadig* himself. Upon which, she shriek'd; and as her Heart was flutter'd between the two Extreams of Transport and Surprize, she fainted away, and gently dropp'd into his Arms. 'Twas, it seems *Astarte* her self; 'twas the Queen of *Babylon*; 'twas the very *Goddess* whom *Zadig* ador'd; 'twas, in short, the very identical Lady, whose hard Fate he had so long deplor'd; and for whose sake he had felt so many agonizing Pains. For a few Minutes he stood speechless, and depriv'd, as it were, of all his senses, whilst his Eyes were fixt on his *Astarte*, who began to revive; and cast a wishful Glance at him, attended with some Confusion. O ye immortal Powers, cried he, who preside over the Destiny of us frail Mortals! Ye have restor'd me my *Astarte*; but alas! at what a Conjuncture, in what a Place, and in what a State and Condition do I view her? He threw himself prostrate on the Ground, and kiss'd the Dust of her Feet. The Queen of *Babylon* rais'd him up, and oblig'd him to sit by her on the flow'ry Bank whereon she was repos'd. Every now and then she wip'd her Eyes, as the Tears trickl'd down afresh her lovely Cheeks. Twenty times she endeavour'd to renew her Discourse; but was interrupted by her Sighs; she ask'd him over and over to relate to her the Hardships he had ran thro' since their parting, and by what Chance he came to traverse that solitary Meadow; but prevented him at the same Time from returning any Answer, by repeating Question upon Question. At last, she gave him a particular Detail of her own Misfortunes, and again requested to know his. Both of them, in short, having, in some Measure, appeas'd the Tumult of their Souls; *Zadig*, in a few Words, inform'd her of the Motives that brought him thither.

But tell me, O unfortunate, tho' ever-venerable Queen, how I came to find you out, reclining on this verdant Bank, dress'd in this servile Habit, accompanied by other Female Slaves, who, I find, have been all Day long in Quest after a *Basilisk*, which, as I understand, is by Order of a celebrated Physician, to be dissolv'd in Rose-water, as a specific Medicine for his dying Patient.

Whilst they busy in their fruitless Search, said the beauteous *Astarte*, I'll tell you the whole Series of Sorrows which I have undergone since last we parted; and since Heav'n has thus unexpectedly blest my Eyes once more with the Sight of my dear *Zadig*, I'll no longer exclaim against my impropitious Stars.

You are not insensible, that the jealous King my Spouse, was disgusted to find you the most amiable of all Mortals, and that for no other Reason he determin'd to strangle you, and poison me. You know very well too, that indulgent Heav'n inspir'd, as it were, my little Dwarf, with artful Means to give me timely Notice of the rash Resolutions of the King, my cruel Husband.

No sooner had the faithful *Cador* oblig'd you to obey my Orders, and to fly the Court, but he ventur'd to enter my Apartment in the Dead of Night thro' a private Door. He snatch'd me up, and convey'd me directly into the Temple of *Orosmades*, where the holy *Magus*, who was his Brother, lock'd me up in that august and awful Statue, that stands erect upon the Pavement of the Temple, and *Colossus*-like, touches the lofty Ceiling with his Head. There I lay conceal'd, or rather buried for some Time; tho' taken all imaginable Care of, and furnish'd with all the Necessaries of Life by that venerable, and loyal Priest. In the mean Time, his Apothecary enter'd at Break of Day into my Apartment, with a Potion in his Hand, compos'd of Opium, black Hellebore, Aconite, and other Ingredients still more baneful. Whilst this mercenary Officer of the King's Vengeance was thus employ'd, another as inhuman as himself, went to your Lodgings with the silken Cord. Both, however, were disappointed, as both of us were fled. *Cador*, very officious, flew to the King, in order the more artfully to blind him; and in a feign'd Passion, rail'd at us both, and charg'd us both as perfidious Traitors. As for that Villain *Zadig*, said he, he has taken his Flight towards *India*; and your false, ungrateful Consort, Sire, said he, is fled to *Memphis*. The Guards were order'd that Moment to pursue us both.

The Couriers, who flew after me, knew nothing of me. I had never expos'd my Face unveil'd to any one but your self, and that too in the Presence, and by the express Order of my Royal Master. As they had no other Marks to distinguish me from others but my Stature, as it had been describ'd, a young Lady, just of my Size, but in all Probability much more handsome, presented herself to their View, on the Frontiers of *Egypt*. She was found alone, and in a very disconsolate Condition. This Lady must, doubtless, said they to themselves, be the Queen of *Babylon*: And without listning to her Complaints, convey'd her instantly to my Husband *Moabdar*. Their gross Blunder at first incens'd his Majesty to the last Degree; but after he had view'd the Lady with an attentive Eye, he found she was extremely pretty, and was soon pacify'd. Her Name was *Missouf.* I have been since inform'd, that her Name in the *Egyptian* Language signifies the *Fair Coquet.* And in Effect, she was so: She had as much Art, however, as Caprice. For she pleas'd the King of Kings: In short, she had such an Ascendancy over him, that he didn't scruple in publick to own her as his Wife. When she had secur'd him thus far in her Toils, she never conceal'd her Power, but play'd the Part of a perfect Humourist. She indulg'd herself in every Whim that came in her Head, without Fear of being brow-beat. In the first Place, She insisted that the Chief Magus, who was old and gouty, should dance a Saraband before her; and upon his modest Refusal to comply with so preposterous a Request, she persecuted him without Mercy: Nothing would serve her Turn, in the next Place, but his Majesty's grand Master of the Horse must make her a Minc'd-pye. The Gentleman took the Liberty to let her know, that he was no profess'd Cook; a Tart, however, he must make for her, and she got him turn'd out of his Place for being so monstrously careless, as to burn one *Corner* of the Crust. Whereupon she gave his Post to her favourite Dwarf, and made her Fop of a Page the Keeper of his Majesty's great Seal, and Confidence. Thus she reign'd arbitrary, and was the Female Tyrant of *Babylon.* All the World deplor'd the Loss of me their former Queen. The King, who never acted the Part of a Tyrant, till the Moment he would have imprison'd me, and strangled you, seem'd to have drown'd all his good Qualities in his Dotage on that capricious Enchantress. He came to the Temple on the solemn Festival of the sacred Fire. I saw him prostrate on the Pavement before the Statue, wherein I was enclos'd, imploring the Gods to show'r down their choicest Blessings on his beauteous *Missouf.* I, with an audible and distinct, but hollow Tone, address'd my self thus, like an Oracle, to the King of Kings. *The Gods reject the Vows of a Monarch, that acts the Tyrant o'er his Subjects; One, who could think of murdering an innocent Wife; and admit of a worthless Beauty to supply her Place.* Moabdar was so startled at this unexpected Answer from the God he ador'd, that he was just at the Point of Distraction. The Oracle that I had deliver'd, and the tyrannical Proceedings of his new Spouse *Missouf,* were enough to deprive him of his Senses. In short, in a few Days he became a perfect Mad-man. Her Caprice, which seem'd a Judgement from above, portended a sudden Revolution. His Subjects accordingly revolted, and were instantly up in Arms. *Babylon,* that had so long indulg'd herself in Indolence and Ease, became the Seat, or Theatre of a bloody Civil War. Whereupon I was taken from my magnificent Prison, the Bowels of his God, and set up at the Head of a very powerful Party. Your Friend *Cador* flew to *Memphis* in hopes to find you there, and bring you back to *Babylon.* The Prince of *Hyrcania,* hearing of these intestine Broils, return'd with a powerful Army, in order to form a third Party, among the *Babylonians.* He attack'd the King, who fled with his fair, but fickle *Egyptian* before him. *Moabdar,* however, was so closely pursu'd, that he dy'd of the Wounds he receiv'd in his Retreat. *Missouf* became the fair Victim of the Conqueror. As for my own Part, I had the Misfortune to be over-power'd likewise, and taken Prisoner by an *Hyrcanian Party,* who brought me into the Presence of the young Prince, at the very Juncture when *Missouf* stood before him. You'll smile, doubtless, when I tell you the Prince look'd upon me as the most amiable Captive of the two; but then, I presume you will be sorry to hear, that my hard Fate doom'd me to be a Vassal in his Seraglio. He told me, in direct Terms, that as soon as he had put an happy Issue to one Military Expedition, which would not, he flatter'd himself, be long unexecuted, he would honour me with a Visit. Judge the dreadful Apprehensions I was under, upon his making such a peremptory Declaration. My Obligations to *Moabdar* were all cancell'd, and I was free to be the Bride of *Zadig*; but instead of that, I fell into the Toils of a *Barbarian*. I answer'd him with all the Resentment becoming one of my high Character and unspotted Virtue. I had always heard say, that Heav'n bestow'd on Persons of my Rank, such a peculiar Mark of Majesty and Grandeur, that with a bare Word, or the Glance of an angry Eye, they could bring down, and abase the Pride of those audacious Creatures that durst to thwart their Inclinations. I talk'd as big as a Queen; but I was treated like the most servile Domestic. The saucy *Hyrcanian*, without so much as vouchsafing me one Single Word, turn'd to his black Eunuch, and told him that I was very impertinent; but yet he could not help thinking I was very pretty. He gave him therefore particular Orders to take care of me, and put me under the same Regimen, with respect to my Diet, as one of his Favourites, in order that I might recover my Colour, which was somewhat too languid; in a Word, that I might become worthy in a little Time of his Royal Favours, and be duely qualified to receive him, when he should honour me so far as to fix the Day. I told him, I would die first: He replied, with a Sneer, that young Ladies, like me, seldom kill'd themselves, and that they were made for Enjoyment; and then turn'd upon his Heel, with as careless an Air, as a Man would part with his Paroquet, when he had shut her up close in her gilded Cage. What a shocking State was I in for the first Queen of the Universe! Nay, I'll say more, for a Heart that was wholly devoted to her *Zadig*!

At these endearing Words, *Zadig* threw himself at her Feet, and bath'd them with his Tears. *Astarte* immediately rais'd him in the most courteous and engaging Manner, and thus continu'd her Narration.—I too plainly perceiv'd, that I was subject to the Tyranny of a *Barbarian*, and the Rival of a Coquet, that was a Slave like myself. She related to me all her past Adventures in *Egypt*. From the Description she gave of her Gallant, the Time and Place, the Dromedary he was mounted on, and from every other minute Circumstance, I imagin'd it was your self that play'd the Hero in her Favour. As I made no Doubt but that you resided somewhere in *Memphis*, I determin'd to go thither my self, but in Disguise. Beauteous *Missouf*, said I, you are of a much sprightlier Disposition than I am; you will be able to amuse the gay young Prince of *Hyrcania* a thousand Times better than I shall. Find out some Way therefore for my Escape; by which you will be sole Lady Regent. You will oblige me to the last Degree, by your friendly Assistance, and at the same Time get rid of a Rival. *Missouf*, (cajol'd with the Hint) came into my Measures directly. She took care to send me packing forthwith, with no other Attendant than an old *Egyptian* Slave.

No sooner had I reach'd the Borders of *Arabia*, but a notorious Free-booter, (one *Arbogad* by Name) pick'd me up, as I was strolling along, and sold me to some Merchants, who convey'd me to yonder Castle, the magnificent Residence of the Emir *Ogul*. He purchas'd me at all Adventures, without enquiring what, or who I was. He is a perfect Debauchee; his sole Delight lies in good Eating, Wine, and Women; and is one, who imagines, that the Almighty sent him into the World for no other Purpose but to gratify his unruly Appetites. He is excessively fat, and puffs and blows every Moment, like one half choak'd. When he has gorg'd himself so unmercifully that he is ready to burst, his chief Physician can persuade him to take any Thing for his Relief; tho' he laughs at him, and despises his Advice when he's well and sober. He has intimated to him, that at present his Life's in Danger, and nothing will restore him but a *Basilisk*, boil'd in Rose-Water. Whereupon the grand *Ogul* has promis'd his last Favours to that Slave, whoever she be, that shall be so fortunate as to catch a *Basilisk*, for him, since it seems they are so seldom to be met with. You see I have others to struggle for the Honour propos'd, and I never had a less Inclination to find out this *Basilisk* than at present, since I have once more met with my dearest *Zadig*.

After this Declaration, *Astarte* and *Zadig* renew'd with Warmth the virtuous Affection which they had long conceiv'd for each other; and reciprocally utter'd all the tenderest Expressions that Love in Distress could possibly devise. And the *Genii*, who preside over all the soft Passions, wafted their mutual Vows of eternal Constancy and Truth to the Sphere of *Venus*.

The whole Train of Slaves, after a long fruitless Search, attended on *Ogul*, to inform him that all their strictest Search was fruitless. *Zadig* desired that he might have the Honour to be introduc'd into his Presence. Accordingly he was, and his Address was to this or the like Effect. May immortal Health descend from Heaven to preserve a Life, Sir, so precious as yours is. I am a Physician by Profession. I flew to your Palace, on the first News of the dangerous Situation you were in, and have brought a *Basilisk* with me, distill'd in Rose-Water. I can have no Hopes of the Honour of your Bed, in Case I succeed in my Application: All the Favour I request, is, the Release of one of your *Babylonish* Slaves, who has been in your Highness's Retinue for some Time. And I am willing to be your Bond-slave in her Stead, if I fail of restoring the most illustrious and magnificent *Ogul* to his pristine State of Health.

The Proposition was readily embrac'd. *Astarte* was instantly discharg'd, and set out for *Babylon*, with a proper Attendant, according to *Zadig*'s Direction; assuring her that she should hear every Day, by a special Courier, of his Proceedings with his new Patient. The Farewel which they took of each other, was very affectionate and tender, expressive of the strongest Obligations to each other. The Moments of Meeting, and those of Parting, are (as it is written in the sacred Book of *Zend*) the two most remarkable *Epochas* of a Lover's Life. *Zadig*'s repeated Protestations of Affection for the Queen were perfectly sincere, and the pure Dictates of his Heart; and the Queen's Love for *Zadig* had made a deeper Impression on hers, than she thought proper to discover.

In the mean Time, *Zadig*, again addressing himself to *Ogul*, said; my *Basilisk*, Sir, as others are, is not to be drest or eaten; but all its Virtues must penetrate your whole Fabrick, thro' your Pores; I have inclos'd my never-failing *Sudorific* in a Bladder, full-blown and carefully cover'd with the softest Leather. You must kick this Bladder, Sir, once a Day about your Hall for a whole Hour together, with all the Vigour and Activity you possibly can. This Medicine must be repeated every Morning, and I'll attend the Operation: Upon your due Observance of the Regimen I shall put you under, I doubt not, but with the Blessing of Heav'n on my honest Endeavours, I shall give you ample Demonstration of my being an Adept in Physick. *Ogul*, upon making the first Experiment, was ready to expire for want of Breath, and thought he should die with the Fatigue. The second Day did not prove altogether so irksome, and he slept much better at Night than he had done before. In short, our Doctor in about eight Days Time, perform'd an absolute Cure. His Patient was as brisk, active and gay, as One in the Bloom of his Youth.

Now, Sir, said *Zadig*, I'll be ingenuous with you, and disclose to you the important Secret. You have play'd at Foot-ball these eight Days successively; and you have liv'd all that Time, within the Bounds of Sobriety and Moderation. Know, Sir, that there is no such Animal in Nature as a *Basilisk*; that Health is to be secur'd by Temperance and Exercise; and that the Art of making Health consistent with Luxury, is altogether as impracticable, and an Art, in all Respects, as idle and chimerical, as those of the Philosopher's Stone, judicial Astrology, or any other Reveries of the like airy and fantastic Nature.

Ogul's Head-Physician, apprehensive that this unexpected Cure, thus wrought by a Stranger, through such an Anti-medicinal Preparation, might possibly not only render himself the Object of Contempt in the Eye of his great Master, but cast a Kind of Slur in general on his whole Fraternity, conven'd a Set of petty Doctors and Apothecaries, who were his Vassals, and entirely devoted to his Interest, to find out some sure Ways and Means to cut off in private his dreadful Rival; but whilst their wicked Plot was hatching, *Zadig* receiv'd a Courier from the Queen *Astarte*.

CHAP. XVI.

The TOURNAMENTS.

T he Queen was receiv'd at *Babylon* with all the Transports of Joy that could possibly be express'd for the safe Return of so illustrious and so beautiful a Personage, that had run thro' such a long Series of Misfortunes. *Babylon* at that Time seem'd to be perfectly serene and quiet. As for the young Prince of *Hyrcania*, he was slain in Battle. The *Babylonians*, who were the Victors, declar'd that *Astarte* should marry that Candidate for the Crown, who should gain it by a fair and impartial Election. They were determin'd, that the most valuable Post of Honour in the World, namely, that of being the Royal Consort of *Astarte*, and the Sovereign of *Babylon*, should be the Result of Merit only; and not be procur'd by any Party-Factions or Court-Intrigues. A solemn Oath was voluntarily taken by all Parties, that he who should distinguish himself by his superior Valour and Wisdom, should unanimously be acknowledg'd the Sovereign-Elect.

A spacious *List*, or *Circus*, was pitched upon, surrounded with commodious Seats, erected in an Amphitheatrical Manner, and richly embellish'd some few Leagues from the City. Thither the Combatants, or Champions were to repair, compleatly accoutred. Each of them had a distinct Apartment to himself behind the *Lists*, where no Soul could either see them, or know who they were. They were to enter the *Lists* four several Times. Those who were so happy as to conquer four Competitors, were afterwards to engage each other in single Combat; in order that he who should remain Master of the Field should be proclaim'd the happy Victor.

Four Days afterwards, they were to meet again, accoutred as before, and to explain all such *Ænigmas*, or *Riddles*, as the *Magi* should think proper to propose. If their Queries should prove too intricate and perplext for them to resolve, they were to have Recourse to the *Lists* again, and after that, to fresh *Ænigmas*, before they could be entitled to the Election: So that the *Tournaments* were to be continu'd till One of the Candidates should be twice a Victor, and shine as conspicuous, with respect to his internal Qualities, as to his Dexterity and Address in heroic Atchievements. The Queen, in the mean Time, was to be narrowly watch'd, and allow'd only to be a Spectator of both their Amusements, at some considerable Distance; and moreover, to be cover'd with a Vail: Nor was she indulg'd so far as to speak one single Word to any Candidate whomsoever, in order to prevent the least Jealousy or Suspicion either of Partiality or Injustice.

Astarte took care, by the Courier, to inform her Lover of all the Preliminary Articles abovemention'd, not doubting but that he would exert both his Courage and Understanding for her Sake, beyond any of the other Competitors.

Zadig accordingly set out for *Babylon*, and besought the Goddess *Venus*, not only to fortify his Courage, but to illuminate his Mind with Wisdom on this important Occasion.

The Night before these martial Atchievements were to commence, *Zadig* arrived upon the Banks of the *Euphrates*. He inscrib'd his Device amongst the List of Combatants; concealing, at the same Time, both his Person and Name, as the Laws of the Election required; and accordingly, withdrew to the Apartment that was provided for him, according to his Lot.

Cador, who was just return'd to *Babylon*, having hunted all *Egypt* over to no Purpose, in Hopes to find his Friend *Zadig*, brought a compleat set of Armour into his Lodge, by express Orders from the Queen: She sent him likewise One of the finest Horses in all *Persia*. *Zadig* knew that these Presents could come from No-body but his dear *Astarte*, which redoubled his Vigour and his Hopes.

The next Morning the Queen being seated under a Canopy of State, enrich'd with precious Stones; and the Amphitheatres being crowded with Gentlemen and Ladies of all Ranks and Conditions from *Babylon*; the Competitors made their personal Appearance in the *Circus*: Each of them went up to the grand *Magus*, and laid down his particular *Device* at his Feet. The *Devices* were drawn by Lot: That of *Zadig* was the last. The first that advanc'd was a Grandee, one *Itabod* by Name, immensely rich, indeed, and very haughty; but no ways couragious; exceedingly awkward, and a Man of no acquir'd Parts. The Sycophants that hover'd round about him flatter'd him, that a Man of his Merit couldn't fail of being King: He imperiously replied, One of my Merit must be King: Whereupon he was arm'd *Cap-a-pee*. His Armour was made of pure Gold, enamell'd with Green. The Housings of his Saddle were green, and his Lance embellish'd with green Ribbands. Every One was sensible, at first Sight, by *Itobad*'s Manner of managing his Horse, that he was not the Man whom Heav'n had pitch'd upon to sway the *Babylonish* Scepter. The first Combatant that tilted with him, threw him out of the Saddle; the second flung him quite over the Crupper, and laid him sprawling on the Ground, with his Heels quiv'ring in the Air. *Itobad*, 'tis true, remounted, but with so ill a Grace, that an universal Laugh went round the Amphitheatre. The third, disdaining to use his Lance, made only a Feint at him: Then catch'd hold of his Right Leg, and whirling him round, threw him flat upon the Sand. The Esquires, who were the Attendants, ran to his Assistance, and with a Sneer remounted him. The fourth Combatant catch'd hold of his Left Leg, and unhors'd him again. He was convey'd thro' the hissing Multitude to his Lodge, where, according to the Law in that Case provided, he was to pass the Night. And as he hobbled along, said he, to the Esquires, what a sad Misfortune is this to One of my Birth and Character!

The other Champions play'd their Parts much better; and all came off with Credit. Some conquer'd two of their Antagonists, and others were so far successful as to get the better of three. None of them, however, except Prince *Hottam*, vanquish'd four. *Zadig*, at last, enter'd the Lists, and dismounted all his four Opponents, one after the other, with the utmost Ease, and with such an Air and Grace, as gain'd him universal Applause. As the Case stood thus, *Zadig* and *Hottam* were to close the Day's Entertainment in a single Combat. The Armour of the latter was of a blue Colour mixt with Gold, and the Housings of his Saddle were of the same. Those of the former white as Snow. The Multitude were divided in their Wishes. The Knight in blue was the Favourite of some of the Ladies; and others again were Admirers of the Cavalier in white. The Queen, whose Heart was in a perfect Palpitation, put up her secret Prayers to *Venus* to assist her darling Hero.

The two Champions making their Passes and their Volta's, with the utmost Dexterity and Address, and keeping firm in their Saddles, gave each other such Rebuffs with their Lances, that all the Spectators (the Queen only excepted) wish'd for two Kings of *Babylon*. At last, their Horses being tired, and both their Lances broke, *Zadig* made use of the following Stratagem, which his Antagonist wasn't any ways appriz'd of. He got artfully behind him, and shooting with a Spring on his Horses Buttocks, grasp'd him close, threw him headlong on the Sand, then jump'd into his Seat, and wheel'd round Prince *Hottam*, while he lay sprawling on the Ground. All the Spectators in general, with loud Acclamations, cried out, Victory! Victory! in favour of the Champion in white. *Hottam*, incens'd to the last Degree, got up, and drew his Sword. *Zadig* sprang from his Horse with his Sabre in his Hand. Now, behold the two Chieftains upon their Legs, commencing a new Trial of Skill! where they seem'd to get the better of each other alternately; for both were strong, and both were active. The Feathers of their Helmets, the Studs of their Bracelets, their Coats of Mail, flew about in Pieces, thro' the dry Blows which they a thousand Times repeated. They struck at each other sometimes with the Edge of their Swords, at other Times they push'd, as Occasion offer'd: Now on the Right, then on the Left; now on the Head, then at the Breast; they retreated; they advanc'd; they kept at a Distance; they clos'd again; they grasp'd each other, turning and twisting like two Serpents, and engag'd each other as fiercely as two *Libyan* Lions fighting for their Prey: Their Swords struck Fire almost at every Blow. At last, *Zadig*, in order to recover his Breath, for a Moment or two stood still, and afterwards, making a Feint at the Prince, threw him on his Back, and disarm'd him. *Hottam*, thereupon, cried out, O thou Knight of the white Armour! 'Tis you only are destin'd to be the King of *Babylon*. The Queen was perfectly transported. The two Champions were reconducted to their separate Lodges, as the others had been before them, in Conformity to the Laws prescrib'd. Several Mutes were order'd to wait on the Champions, and carry them some proper Refreshment. We'll leave the Reader to judge whether the Queen's Dwarf was not appointed to wait on *Zadig* on this happy Occasion. After Supper the Mutes withdrew, and left the Combatants to rest their wearied Limbs till the next Morning; at which Time the Victor was to produce his *Device*, before the *Grand Magus*, in order to confer Notes, and discover the Hero whoever he might be.

Zadig slept very sound, notwithstanding his amorous Regard for the Queen, being perfectly fatigu'd. *Itabod*, who lay in the Lodge contiguous to his, could not once close his Eyes for Vexation. He got up therefore in the Dead of the Night, stole imperceptibly into *Zadig*'s Apartment, took his white Armour and Device away with him, and substituted his green One in its Place.

As soon as the Day began to dawn, he repair'd, with a seemingly undaunted Courage, to the *Grand Magus*, to inform him, that he was the mighty Hero, the happy Victor. Without the least Hesitation, he gain'd his Point, and was proclaim'd Victor before *Zadig* was awake. *Astarte*, astonish'd at this unexpected Disappointment, return'd with a Heart overwhelm'd with Despair, to the Court of *Babylon*. Almost all the Spectators were mov'd off from the Amphitheatre before *Zadig* wak'd: He hunted for his Arms; but could find nothing but those in green. He was oblig'd, tho' sorely against his Will, to put it on, having nothing else in his Lodge to appear in: Confounded, and big with Resentment, he drest himself, and made his personal Appearance in that despicable Equipage. The Populace that were left behind in the *Circus*, hiss'd him every Step he took, they made a Ring about him, and treated him with all the Marks of Ignominy and Contempt. The most cowardly Wretch breathing was never sure so sweated, or hunted down as poor *Zadig*! He grew quite out of Patience at last, and cut his Way thro' the insulting Mob, with his Rival's Sabre; but he did not know what Measures to pursue, or how to rectify so gross a Mistake. It was not in his Power to have a Sight of the Queen; he could never recover the white Armour again which She had sent him; That was the Compromise, or the Engagement, to which the Combatants had all unanimously agreed: Thus, as he was on the one Hand, plung'd in an Abyss of Sorrow; so on the other, he was almost drove distracted with Vexation and Resentment. He withdrew therefore, in a solitary Mood, to the Banks of the *Euphrates*, now fully persuaded, that his impropitious Star had shed its most baleful Influence on him, and that his Misfortunes were irretrievable, revolving in his Mind, all his Disappointments from his first Adventure with the Court-Coquet, who had entertain'd an utter Aversion to a blind Eye, down to his late Loss of his white Armour. See! said he, the fatal Consequence of being a Sluggard! Had I been more vigilant, I had been King of *Babylon*; but what is more, I had been happy in the Embraces of my dearest *Astarte*. All the Knowledge of Books or Mankind; all the personal Valour that I can boast of, has only prov'd an Aggravation of my Sorrows. He carried the Point so far at last, as to murmur at the unequal Dispensations of Divine Providence; and was tempted to believe, that all Occurrences were govern'd by a malignant Destiny, which never fail'd to oppress the Virtuous, and always crown'd the Actions of such Villains as the green Knight, with uncommon Success. In one of his frantick Fits, he put on the green Armour, that had created him such a World of Disgrace. A Merchant happening to pass by, he sold it to him for a Trifle, and took in Exchange nothing more than a Mantle, and a Cap. In this Disguise, he took a solitary Walk along the Banks of the *Euphrates*, every Minute reflecting in his Mind on the partial Proceedings of Providence, which never ceas'd to torment him.

CHAP. XVII.

The HERMIT.

A s *Zadig* was travelling along, he met with a Hermit, whose grey and venerable Beard descended to his Girdle. He had in his Hand a little Book, on which his Eyes were fix'd. *Zadig* threw himself in his Way, and made him a profound Bow. The Hermit return'd the Compliment with such an Air of Majesty and Benevolence, that *Zadig*'s Curiosity prompted him to converse with so agreeable a Stranger. Pray, Sir, said he, what may be the Contents of the Treatise you are reading with such Attention. 'Tis call'd, said the Hermit, the *Book of Fate*; will you please to look at it. He put the Book into the Hands of *Zadig*, who, tho' he was a perfect Master of several Languages, couldn't decypher one single Character. This rais'd his Curiosity still higher. You seem dejected, said the good Father to him. Alas! I have Cause enough, said *Zadig*. If you'll permit me to accompany you, said the old Hermit, perhaps I may be of some Service to you. I have sometimes instill'd Sentiments of Consolation into the Minds of the Afflicted. *Zadig* had a secret Regard for the Air of the old Man, for his Beard, and his Book. He found, by conversing with him, that he was the most learned Person he had ever met with. The Hermit harangu'd on Destiny, Justice, Morality, the sovereign Good, the Frailty of Nature; on Virtue and Vice, in such a lively Manner, and in such a Flow of Words, that *Zadig* was attach'd to him by an invincible Charm. He begg'd earnestly that he would favour him with his Company to *Babylon*. That Favour I was going to ask my self, said the old Man. Swear to me by *Orosmades*, that you won't leave me, for some Days at least, let me do what I please. *Zadig* took the Oath requir'd, and both pursu'd their Journey.

The two Travellers arriv'd that Evening at a superb Castle. The Hermit begg'd for an hospitable Reception of himself and his young Comrade. The Porter, whom any One might have taken for some Grandee, let them in, but with a kind of Coldness and Contempt. However, he conducted them to the Head-Steward, who went with them thro' every rich Apartment of his Master's House. They were seated at Supper afterwards at the lower End, indeed, of the Table, and where they were taken little or no Notice of by the Host; but they were serv'd with as much Delicacy and Profusion, as any of the other Guests. When they arose from Table, they wash'd their Hands in a Golden Bason set with Emeralds, and other costly Stones. When 'twas Time to go to Rest, they were conducted into a Bed-chamber richly furnish'd; and the next Morning two Pieces of Gold were presented to him for their mutual Service, by a Valet in waiting; and then they were dismiss'd.

The Proprietor of this Castle, said *Zadig*, as they were upon the Road, seems to me to be a very hospitable Gentleman; tho' somewhat too haughty indeed, and too imperious: The Words were no sooner out of his Mouth, but he perceiv'd that the Pocket of his Comrade's Garment, tho' very large, was swell'd, and greatly extended: He soon saw what was the Cause, and that he had clandestinely brought off the Golden Laver. He durst not immediately take Notice of the Fact; but was ready to sink at the very Thoughts on't. About Noon, the Hermit rapp'd at a petty Cottage with his Staff, the beggarly Residence of an old, rich Miser. He desir'd that he and his Companion might refresh themselves there for a few Hours. An old, shabby Domestick let them in indeed, but with visible Reluctance, and carried them into the Stable, where all their Fare was a few musty Olives, and a Draught or two of sower small Beer. The Hermit seem'd as content with his Repast, as he was the Night before. At last, rising off from his Seat, he paid his Compliments to the old Valet (who had as watchful an Eye over them all the Time, as if they had been a Brace of Thieves, and intimated every now and then that he fear'd they would be benighted) and gave him the two Pieces of Gold, he had but just receiv'd that Morning, as a Token of his Gratitude for his courteous Entertainment. He added moreover, I would willingly speak one Word with your Master before I go. The Valet, thunder-struck at his unexpected Gratuity, comply'd with his Request: Most hospitable Sir, said the Hermit, I couldn't go away without returning you my grateful Acknowledgments for the friendly Reception we have met with this Afternoon. Be pleas'd to accept this Golden Bason as a small Token of my Gratitude and Esteem. The Miser started, and was ready to fall down backwards at the Sight of so valuable a Present. The Hermit gave him no Time to recover out of his Surprise, but march'd off that Moment with his young Comrade. Father, said *Zadig*, What is all this that I have seen? You seem to me to act in a quite different Manner from the Generality of Mankind. You plunder One, who entertain'd you with all the Pomp and Profusion in the World, to enrich a covetous, sordid Wretch, who treated you in the most unworthy Manner. Son, said the old Man, that Grandee, who receives Visits of Strangers, with no other View than to gratify his Pride, and to raise their Astonishment at the Furniture of his Palace, will henceforward learn to be wiser; and the Miser to be more liberal for the Time to come. Don't be surpris'd, but follow me. *Zadig* was at a stand at present; and couldn't well determine whether his Companion was a Man of greater Wisdom than ordinary, or a Mad-man. But the Hermit assum'd such an Ascendency over him, exclusive of the Oath he had taken, that he couldn't tell how to leave him. At Night they came to a House very commodiously built, but neat and plain; where nothing was wanting, and yet nothing profuse. The Master was a Philosopher, that had retir'd from the busy World, in order to live in Peace, and form his Mind to Virtue. He was pleas'd to build this little

Box for the Reception of Strangers, in a handsome Manner, but without Ostentation. He came in Person to meet them at the Door, and for a Time, advis'd them to sit down and rest themselves in a commodious Apartment. After some Respite, he invited them to a frugal, yet elegant Repast; during which, he talk'd very intelligently about the late Revolutions in *Babylon*. He seem'd entirely to be in the Queen's Interest, and heartily wish'd that *Zadig* had entred the Lists for the regal Prize: But *Babylon*, said he, don't deserve a King of so much Merit. A modest Blush appear'd in *Zadig*'s Face at this unexpected Compliment, which innocently aggravated his Misfortunes. It was agreed, on all Hands, that the Affairs of this World took sometimes a quite different Turn from what the wisest Patriots would wish them. The Hermit replied, the Ways of Providence are often very intricate and obscure, and Men were much to blame for casting Reflections on the Conduct of the Whole, upon the bare Inspection of the minutest Part.

The next Topick they entred upon was the Passions. Alas! said *Zadig*, how fatal in their Consequences! However, said the Hermit, they are the Winds that swell the Sail of the Vessel. Sometimes, 'tis true, they overset it; but there is no such Thing as sailing without them. Phlegm, indeed, makes Men peevish and sick; but then there is no living without it. Tho' every Thing here below is dangerous, yet All are necessary.

In the next Place, their Discourse turn'd on sensual Pleasures; and the Hermit demonstrated, that they were the Gifts of Heaven; for, said he, Man cannot bestow either Sensations or Ideas on himself; he receives them all; his Pain and Pleasure, as well as his Being, proceed from a superior Cause.

Zadig stood astonish'd, to think how a Man that had committed such vile Actions, could argue so well on such Moral Topicks. At the proper Hour, after an Entertainment, not only instructive, but ev'ry way agreeable, their Host conducted them to their Bed-chamber, thanking Heaven for directing two such polite and virtuous Strangers to his House. He offer'd them at the same Time some Silver, to defray their Expences on the Road; but with such an Air of Respect and Benevolence, that 'twas impossible to give the least Disgust. The Hermit, however, refus'd it, and took his leave, as he propos'd to set forward for *Babylon* by Break of Day. Their Parting was very affectionate and friendly; *Zadig*, in particular, express'd a more than common Regard for a Man of so amiable a Behaviour. When the Hermit and he were alone, and preparing for Bed, they talk'd long in Praise of their new Host. As soon as Day-light appear'd, the old Hermit wak'd his young Comrade. 'Tis Time to be gone, said he; but as all the House are fast asleep, I'll leave a Token behind me of my Respect and Affection for the Master of it. No sooner were the Words out of his Mouth, but he struck a Light, kindled a Torch, and set the

Building in a Flame: *Zadig*, in the utmost Confusion, shriek'd out, and would, if possible, have prevented him from being guilty of such a monstrous Act of Ingratitude. The Hermit dragg'd him away, by a superior Force. The House was soon in a Blaze: When they had got at a convenient Distance, the Hermit, with an amazing Sedateness, turn'd back and survey'd the destructive Flames. Behold, said he, our fortunate Friend! In the Ruins, he will find an immense Treasure, that will enable him, from henceforth, to exert his Beneficence, and render his Virtues more and more conspicuous. *Zadig*, tho' astonish'd to the last Degree, attended him to their last Stage, which was to the Cottage of a very virtuous and well-dispos'd Widow, who had a Nephew of about fourteen Years of Age. He was a hopeful Youth, and the Darling of her Heart. She entertain'd her two Guests with the best Provisions her little House afforded. In the Morning she order'd her Nephew to attend them to an adjacent Bridge, which, having been broken down some few Days before, render'd the Passage dangerous to Strangers.

The Lad, being very attentive to wait on them, went formost. When they were got upon the Bridge; come hither, my pretty Boy, said the Hermit, I must give your Aunt some small Token of my Respect for her last Night's Favours. Upon that, he twisted his Fingers in the Hair of his Head, and threw him, very calmly, into the River. Down went the little Lad; he came up once again to the Surface of the Water; but was soon lost in the rapid Stream. O thou Monster! thou worst of Villains, cry'd *Zadig*! Didn't you promise, said the Hermit, to view my Conduct with Patience? Know then, that had that Boy liv'd but one Year longer, he would have murder'd his Foster-Mother. Who told you so, you barbarous Wretch, said *Zadig*? And when did you read that inhuman Event in your *Black-Book* of *Fate*? Who gave you Permission pray, to drown so innocent a Youth, that had never disoblig'd you?

No sooner had our young *Babylonian* ceas'd his severe Reflections, but he perceiv'd that the old Hermit's long Beard grew shorter and shorter; that the Furrows in his Face began to fill up, and that his Cheeks glow'd with a Rose-coloured Red, as if he had been in the Bloom of Fifteen. His Mantle was vanish'd at once; and on his Shoulders, which were before cover'd, appear'd four angelic Wings, each refulgent as the Sun. O thou Messenger of Heaven! O thou angelic Form! cry'd *Zadig*, and fell prostrate at his Feet; thou art descended from the Empireum, I find, to instruct such a poor frail Mortal as I am, how to submit to the Mysteries of Fate. Mankind in general, said the Angel *Jesrad*, judge of the Whole, by only viewing the hither Link of the Chain. Thou, of all the human Race, wast the only Man that deserv'd to have thy Mind enlighten'd. *Zadig*, begg'd Leave to speak. I am somewhat diffident of myself, 'tis true; but may I presume, Sir, to beg the Solution of one Scruple? Would it not have been better to have chastiz'd the Lad, and by that

Means reform'd him, than to have cut him off thus unprepar'd in a Moment. *Jesrad*, replied, had he been virtuous, and had he liv'd, 'twas his *Fate* not only to be murder'd himself, but his Wife, whom he would afterwards have married, and the little Infant, that was to have been the Pledge of their mutual Affection. Is it necessary then, venerable Guide, that there should be Wickedness and Misfortunes in the World, and that those Misfortunes should fall with Weight on the Heads of the Righteous? The Wicked, replied *Jesrad*, are always unhappy. Misfortunes are intended only as a Touch-stone, to try a small Number of the Just, who are thinly scatter'd about this terrestrial Globe: Besides, there is no Evil under the Sun, but some Good proceeds from it: But, said *Zadig*, Suppose the World was all Goodness, and there was no such Thing in Nature as Evil. Then, that World of yours, said *Jesrad*, would be another World; the Chain of Events would be another Wisdom; and that other Order, which would be perfect, must of Necessity be the everlasting Residence of the supreme Being, whom no Evil can approach. That great and first Cause has created an infinite Number of Worlds, and no two of them alike. This vast Variety is an Attribute of his Omnipotence. There are not two Leaves on the Trees throughout the Universe, nor any two Globes of Light amongst the Myriad of Stars that deck the infinite Expanse of Heaven, which are perfectly alike. And whatever you see on that small Atom of Earth, whereof you are a Native, must exist in the Place, and at the Time appointed, according to the immutable Decrees of him who comprehends the Whole. Mankind imagine, that the Lad, whom I plung'd into the River, was drown'd by *Chance*; and that our generous Benefactor's House was reduc'd to Ashes by the same *Chance*; but know, there is no such Thing as *Chance*, all Misfortunes are intended, either as severe Trials, Judgments, or Rewards; and are the Result of Foreknowledge. You remember, Sir, the poor Fisherman in Despair, that thought himself the most unhappy Mortal breathing. The great *Orasmades*, sent you to amend his Situation. Frail Mortal! Cease to contend with what you ought to adore. But, said *Zadig*—whilst the Sound of the Word But dwelt upon his Tongue, the Angel took his Flight towards the tenth Sphere. *Zadig* sunk down upon his Knees, and acknowledg'd an over-ruling Providence with all the Marks of the profoundest Submission. The Angel, as he was soaring towards the Clouds, cried out in distinct Accents; Make thy Way towards *Babylon*.

CHAP. XVIII.

The ÆNIGMAS, or RIDDLES.

*Z*adig, as one beside himself, and perfectly thunder-struck, beat his March at random. He entred, however, into the City of *Babylon*, on that very Day, when those Combatants who had been before engag'd in the List or Circus, were already assembled in the spacious Outer-Court of the Palace, in order to solve the Ænigmas, and give the wisest Answers they could to such Questions, as the *Grand Magus* should propose. All the Parties concern'd were present, except the Knight of the Green Armour. No sooner had *Zadig* made his Appearance in the City, but the Populace flock'd round about him: No Eye was satisfied with gazing at him: All in general were lavish of their Praises, and in their Hearts wish'd him their Sovereign, except the envious Man, who as he pass'd by, fetch'd a deep Sigh, and turn'd his Head aside. The Populace with loud Acclamations attended him to the Palace-Gate. The Queen, who had heard of his Arrival, was in the utmost Agony, between Hope and Despair. Her Vexation had almost brought her to Death's Door; she couldn't conceive why *Zadig* should appear without his Accoutrements, nor imagine which Way *Itobad* could procure the snow-white Armour. At the Sight of *Zadig* a confus'd Murmur ran thro' the whole Place. Every Eye was surpriz'd, tho' charm'd at the same Time to see him again: But then none were to be admitted into the Assembly-Room except the Knights.

I have fought as successfully as any one of them all, said *Zadig*, tho' another appears clad in my Armour; but in the mean Time, before I can possibly prove my Assertion, I insist upon being admitted into Court, in order to give my Solutions to such Ænigmas as shall be propos'd. 'Twas put to the Vote. As the Reputation of his being a Man of the strictest Honour and Veracity was so strongly imprinted on their Minds, the Motion of his Admittance was carried in the Affirmative, without the least Opposition.

The first Question the *Grand Magus* propos'd was this: What is the longest and yet the shortest Thing in the World; the most swift and the most slow; the most divisible, and the most extended; the least valu'd, and the most regretted; And without which nothing can possibly be done: Which, in a Word, devours every Thing how minute soever, and yet gives Life and Spirit to every Object or Being, however Great?

Itobad had the Honour to answer first. His reply was, that a Man of his Merit had something else to think on, than idle Riddles; 'twas enough for him, that he was acknowledg'd the Hero of the Circus. One said, the Solution of the

Ænigma propos'd was *Fortune*; others said the *Earth*; and others again the *Light*: But *Zadig* pronounced it to be *Time*. Nothing, said he, can be longer, since 'tis the Measure of Eternity; Nothing is shorter, since there is Time always wanting to accomplish what we aim at. Nothing passes so slowly as Time to him who is in Expectation; and nothing so swift as Time to him who is in the perfect Enjoyment of his Wishes. It's Extent is to Infinity, in the Whole; and divisible to Infinity in part. All Men neglect it in the Passage; and all regret the Loss of it when 'tis past. Nothing can possibly be done without it; it buries in Oblivion whatever is unworthy of being transmitted down to Posterity; and it renders all illustrious Actions immortal. The Assembly agreed unanimously that *Zadig* was in the Right.

The next Question that was started, was, What is the Thing we receive, without being ever thankful for it; which we enjoy, without knowing how we came by it; which we give away to others, without knowing where 'tis to be found; and which we lose, without being any ways conscious of our Misfortune?

Each pass'd his Verdict. *Zadig* was the only Person that concluded it was LIFE. He solv'd every Ænigma propos'd, with equal Facility. *Itobad*, when he heard the Explications, always said that nothing in the World was more easy, than to solve such obvious Questions; and that he could interpret a thousand of them without the least Hesitation, were he inclin'd to trouble his Head about such Trifles. Other Questions were propos'd in regard to Justice, the sovereign Good, and the Art of Government. *Zadig*'s Answers still carried the greatest Weight. What Pity 'tis, said some who were present, that one of so comprehensive a Genius, should make such a scurvy Cavalier?

Most illustrious Grandees, said *Zadig*, I was the Person that had the Honour of being Victor at your Circus; the white Armour, most puissant Lords, was mine. That awkward Warrior there, Lord *Itobad*, dress'd himself in it whilst I was asleep. He imagin'd, it is plain, that it would do him more Honour than his own Green one. Unaccoutred as I am, I am ready, before this august Assembly, to give them incontestable Proof of my superior Skill; to engage with the Usurper of the White Armour with my Sword only in my Mantle and Bonnet; and to testify that I only was the happy Victor of the justly admired *Hottam*.

Itobad accepted of the Challenge with all the Assurance of Success imaginable. He did not doubt, but being properly accoutred with his Helmet, his Cuirass, and his Bracelets, he should be able to hue down an Antagonist, in his Mantle and Cap, and nothing to skreen him from his Resentment, but a single Sabre. *Zadig* drew his Sword, and saluted the Queen with it, who view'd him with Transport mix'd with Fear. *Itobad* drew his, but paid his

Compliments to Nobody. He approach'd *Zadig*, as one, whom he imagin'd incapable of making any considerable Resistance. He concluded, 'twas in his Power to cut *Zadig* into Atoms. *Zadig*, however, knew how to parry the Blow, by dexterously receiving it upon his *Fort* (as the Swords-men call it) by which Means *Itobad*'s Sword was snapt in two. With that *Zadig* in an Instant clos'd his Adversary, and by his superior Strength, as well as Skill, laid him sprawling on his Back. Then holding the Point of his Sword to the opening of his Cuirass, Submit to be stripp'd of your borrow'd Plumes, or you are a dead Man this Moment. *Itobad*, always surpriz'd, that any Disappointment should attend a Man of such exalted Merit as himself, very tamely permitted *Zadig* to disrobe him by Degrees of his pompous Helmet, his superb Cuirass, his rich Bracelets, his brilliant Cuisses, or Armour for his Thighs, and other Martial Accoutrements. When *Zadig* had equipp'd himself *Cap-a-pee*, in his now recover'd Armour, he flew to *Astarte*, and threw himself prostrate at her Feet. *Cador* prov'd, without any great Difficulty, that the White Armour was *Zadig*'s Property. He was thereupon acknowledg'd King of *Babylon*, by the unanimous Content of the Whole Court; but more particularly with the Approbation of *Astarte*, who after such a long Series of Misfortunes, now tasted the Sweets of seeing her darling *Zadig* thought worthy, in the Opinion of the whole World, to be the Partner of her royal Bed. *Itobad* withdrew, and contented himself with being call'd *my Lord* within the narrow Compass of his own Domesticks. *Zadig*, in short, was elected King, and was as happy as any Mortal could be.

Now he began to reflect on what the Angel *Jesrad* had said to him: Nay, he reflected so far back as the Story of the *Arabian* Atom of Dust metamorphosed into a Diamond. The Queen and He ador'd the Divine Providence. *Zadig* permitted *Missouf*, the Fair Coquet, to make her Conquests where she could. He sent Couriers to bring the Free-booter *Arbogad* to Court, and gave him an Honourable Military Post in his Army, with a farther Promise of Promotion to the highest Dignity; but upon this express Condition, that he would act for the future as a Soldier of Honour; but assur'd him at the same Time, that he'd make a publick Example of him, if he follow'd his Profession of Free-booting for the future.

Setoc was sent for from the lonely Desarts of *Arabia*, together with the fair *Almonza*, his new Bride, to preside over the commercial Affairs of *Babylon*. *Cador* was advanc'd to a Post near himself, and was his Favourite Minister at Court, as the just Reward of his past Services. He was, in short, the King's real Friend; and *Zadig* was the only Monarch in the Universe that could boast of such an Attendant. The Dwarf, tho' dumb, was not wholly forgotten. The Fisherman was put into the Possession of a very handsome House; and *Orcan* was sentenc'd, not only to pay him a very considerable Sum for the Injustice done him in detaining his Wife; but to resign her likewise to the proper Owner: The Fisherman, however, grown wise by Experience, soften'd the Rigour of the Sentence, and took the Money only in full of all Accounts.

He didn't leave so much as *Semira* wholly disconsolate, tho' she had such an Aversion to a blind Eye; nor *Azora* comfortless, notwithstanding her affectionate Intention to shorten his Nose; for he sooth'd their Sorrows by very munificent Presents. The envious Informer indeed, died with Shame and Vexation. The Empire was glorious abroad, and in the full Enjoyment of Tranquility, Peace and Plenty, at home: This, in short, was the true golden Age. The whole Country was sway'd by Love and Justice. Every one blest *Zadig*; and *Zadig* blest Heav'n for his unexpected Success.

FINIS.